D0292816

WESTERN JUSTICE . . .

Longarm drew his bead and squeezed lightly on the trigger of the Winchester. The carbine rocked back against his shoulder with a satisfying bellow, and the man below and in front of him clutched his groin and spun around before falling.

Whatever he had had between his legs was gone now, torn away by a .44 caliber chunk of friction-heated lead and smashed into the ground behind him.

Quickly Longarm levered another cartridge into the chamber and called out, "The rest of you sit right where you are."

The man who had been shot screamed and began to flop back and forth . . .

TABOR EVANS

LONGARM

AND THE COTTONWOOD CURSE

A JOVE BOOK

LONGARM AND THE COTTONWOOD CURSE

A Jove Book/published by arrangement with
the author

PRINTING HISTORY
Jove edition/May 1987

ISBN: 0-515-08959-1

Chapter 1

Deputy U.S. Marshal Custis Long ambled into the U.S. marshal's office in the federal building very nearly on time —not more than fifteen or twenty minutes late, anyway. He had a half-smoked cheroot clamped between his teeth and a satisfied look about him.

"Longarm!" Henry greeted him from behind his desk. Henry was the chief clerk for Marshal Billy Vail. Henry was *always* on time. Damn well often was early to work, Longarm believed, although he was seldom around to verify that. "You're early," the clerk went on.

Longarm raised an eyebrow and made a show of checking the timepiece at one end of his watch chain. The other end of that chain held a small derringer which he did not display quite so readily as he did the watch. "Damn, Henry, you really are turned around this morning. I'm eighteen minutes late. Besides which, you sound glad to

1

see me. *That* sure ain't normal. You want me to go get you some salts or something?"

"No, but we didn't expect to see you for several days."

The "we" of course, would be Henry and Marshal Vail. That much Longarm could figure. But old Henry being pleased to see him? Now that was something.

"You mean that business with Hootmon? Nothing to it, Henry. The man had himself a mistress. That's what got him in trouble to begin with, trying to keep her happy and buy his way out o' the guilts with his wife too. Soon as he heard there was a warrant out on him he went runnin' to the girl friend for comfort. I just scooped him up—hell, he's one of them eyeshade thieves, not the rough kind; he didn't offer any fuss about it when I held the cuffs out to him—and put the both of us on the next train east. No problem. I got in last night, turned him over to competent authority." Longarm began to dig into his coat pockets. "I got the receipt for him here someplace. There it is." He pulled it out, unfolded it to make sure that he hadn't grabbed some young lady's address by mistake, and turned it over to Henry for filing, or whatever Henry did with all the paperwork the working folks had to turn in around here.

"Well, I am certainly glad to see you back so soon," Henry said. He laid the prisoner receipt form on top of his desk, which was as tidy and unsullied as the inside of a spinster's drawers, and fussily tried to straighten out the wrinkles and creases the paper had developed in Longarm's pockets.

"I could go out and see can I find a flatiron to help you there, Henry, but I don't know as I could get it here hot enough for you," Longarm offered.

Henry gave him a dirty look but went right on with what he was doing. "The marshal will want to see you right away."

Longarm grinned at him and pushed his jaw forward a

little to tilt the tip of his cheroot to a jaunty angle. "Hey, Henry, you said yourself that I'm not due back for a couple days yet. There's some things I could be doing while you boys wait for me to report in."

One of those things, though he couldn't see any reason to discuss it with Henry, was the reason he was a tad late this morning. That reason was dark-haired and green-eyed and served breakfasts at the Brown Palace, where Longarm had just been. The fact that she served breakfasts likely meant that she had her evenings free. He'd had a nice little chat with her over his ham and eggs and was thinking that more conversation could be called for, a notion that she had seemed to be encouraging without actually quite saying so.

"Don't be getting any ideas," Henry warned. "The boss has been pacing the floor waiting for you practically since you left."

"C'mon, Henry. There's other deputies in this office. You don't have to interfere with my social life every damn time I get something lined up close to home."

Henry glanced toward the closed door leading into Marshal Billy Vail's office, then leaned forward and whispered —like it was some big damn secret that Longarm wouldn't hear about for himself in a couple of minutes anyway—"Special request. Very high up and very official, Longarm."

Longarm was unimpressed. Very high, very official requests were usually something really interesting, like a visiting senator with a fat daughter who needed escorting around the sights of Denver.

He saw that the ash on the end of his cheroot was getting long, so he leaned forward over Henry's desk and— quite by accident, of course—wiggled his jaw a little when he whispered back, "Whatever you say, Henry." The ash was dislodged and landed squarely in the center of the polished wood. Longarm appeared not to have noticed, but

3

Henry almost went into a tizzy trying to sweep away the offensive stuff.

"Should I go in now?" Longarm asked. "Or do you want me to see can I guess what's up?"

Henry gave him a sourly suspicious look, both of them knowing full well that the clerk was never going to be able to prove that the ash dropping had been deliberate, and motioned him toward the closed door.

"Thanks." Longarm hung his brown Stetson on the hat rack, smoothed back his hair, and presented himself inside the boss's office.

Billy Vail was behind his desk, bent over a pile of papers, more of the avalanche of paperwork that only he and Henry seemed to understand—if even they did—but he put that aside with a genuinely pleased welcome when he saw who was intruding on his work.

Longarm had to go through the line of explanations all over again for him.

"I'm glad to hear that, Longarm. No troubles, you say?"

"Naw."

"Good. Very good. Have a seat over there. Make yourself comfortable. Drink?"

At this hour of morning? Uh-oh, Longarm thought. Whatever was coming, he wasn't going to like it. He could tell that right away. It was probably a cabinet member with *two* fat daughters he'd have to squire around town.

Longarm took the indicated seat and waited patiently while Billy Vail pushed one pile of papers aside and replaced them with a folder from the top drawer of his big desk. The marshal was getting more than a bit bald and paunchy nowadays, but he used to be one hell of a field man back in his day. Longarm began to feel just a little bit better. A file folder like that usually meant real work, and any damn thing would be better than social duty.

"I have a special request for your particular services," Billy Vail told him.

"Oh, I can believe that," Longarm said. "From some fine-looking lady, no doubt. A man's reputation does tend to spread far and wide." He grinned, but Billy Vail was all business this morning.

"This particular request comes from the Bureau of Indian Affairs. The Bureau for some reason, believes that your reputation precedes you. Although personally I pray constantly that it does not." He said that straight-faced too, darn him, Longarm noticed.

"The Sioux aren't getting nervous again, are they, Billy?" Longarm had heard no rumors about that lately, but then he had been out of town for several days. He was already thinking of old friendships made in the line of past duties, tribal leaders whose influence he might be able to call on if there was another reservation break being planned up north.

"No, this has nothing to do with the Sioux," Vail said. "Kiowa-Apache."

Longarm frowned. "I know some Kiowa. And I've run into a few Apache. Who the hell are the Kiowa-Apache?"

Billy Vail grunted. "I've run into a few of *them* before, but never one to talk to. They were always at the other end of a rifle barrel when I saw them."

In his younger days Vail had spent time as a Texas Ranger and done his fair share of Indian fighting.

"Rough boys?" Longarm asked.

"Very. Funny bunch. Bright too. Not set in their ways and hanging onto traditions like most tribes do. According to this BIA report, they're some kind of offshoot tribe, not fish and not quite fowl either. They've been running with the Kiowas for a hundred years or so, if you can believe the scientific types who make a big thing out of studying such, but they speak a version of the Apache language. I don't know anything about that, but I can tell you that they are a tricky bunch when they get their dander up. They can handle a horse as well as any Kiowa, and they're as mean

5

as their Apache ancestors. Before they come at you they lay back and figure out what they think will work. And, believe me, they raise a lot of hair when they want to."

Longarm grunted and stubbed his cheroot out on the sole of his boot. "If the Bureau wants me because I can talk to some Indians, I hope they don't think I can talk to *every* Indian. I don't guess I know more'n a few words of Nadene."

"I wish it was that simple," Vail said. "The deal is this. The Kiowa-Apache have been put on their own reservation down near the Guadalupes."

Longarm groaned a little. That was one hot part of the country, and this was coming into the hot time of the year —which even January could be down there. In the summer, a man might as well lay out his bedroll in a furnace as tramp around in West Texas.

"I said they were bright," Vail went on. "They are wanting to jump into civilization, at least according to the BIA, if you can believe them. They are willing to adopt civilized ways, which is certainly more than you can say for many tribes, so they have been given a reservation of their own and seed herds of cattle and sheep to raise. The idea is that the tribe should be self-supporting within a few years and everybody be happier for it."

"That sounds sensible enough. What's the problem?"

Vail frowned down toward the BIA report as if he were accusing it of something. "That's what I'm getting to," he said in a complaining tone of voice. "There may be some jurisdictional difficulties with this one, Longarm. The Kiowa-Apache reservation is federal territory, of course, under the direction of a BIA agent. I have a letter of introduction here for you to take." Billy sighed and rubbed a palm over the barren and somewhat shiny top of his head. "Then there are the state authorities in Texas to deal with. And much of the area around the reservation is in New Mexico Territory, with territorial government to deal with."

6

"Damn it, Billy, that's all real interesting, but what the hell is the *problem?*"

Vail scowled. The poor man looked like he wanted to spit—at Longarm, if he was the only victim he could find.

"A curse," he snapped.

"Come again, Billy? I don't reckon I heard that right."

"You heard me, damn it. There is supposed to be some kind of curse on that area."

"A curse," Longarm repeated slowly. He pulled a fresh cheroot out and admired the end of it for a bit. "You're telling me that these Kiowa-Apache, who you say are so bright and suddenly civilized, are scared there is a curse on their reservation?"

Vail sighed. "Actually," he admitted, "the Kiowa-Apache *like* the damn reservation." He sighed again, louder this time. "Actually, it's the *Texans* who are saying there is a curse. They claim the Indians put this curse on them and are killing them with it. They're the ones who want the reservation moved. Or the Kiowa-Apache killed. I gather they don't much care which."

Longarm would have laughed, except that he knew poor Billy was serious about this. So instead he sat there and stared at his boss for a minute or so. "You want me to . . . uh . . ."

"The Bureau of Indian Affairs, officially, would like you to mosey down to Cottonwood, Texas, and remove the curse. Please." Vail snapped a fingernail on the crisp paper of the report he was holding.

"Right," Longarm said sarcastically. "Do they say *how* I should I do that? Magic powders, maybe? Any incantations recommended?"

Billy gave him a dirty look.

This time it was Deputy United States Marshal Custis Long who did the sighing. "Right," he repeated. "I'll get right on it, Billy. Curses removed on demand. No problem. Whatever they want." He shook his head. "Curse, huh?"

Chapter 2

There were any number of ways to get down to the reservation, but none of them was any good. That area down around the Guadalupes was one of those places where, like the fellow said, you just couldn't hardly get there from here. No matter where you were starting out from.

Longarm chewed on that problem some while he went home to his rented room and got the bag he always kept ready for unexpected travel. He had just gotten in last night and had not yet had time to get any laundry done. He wouldn't have time to have it done before he left, either, so he settled for making do with what was handy and didn't smell completely ripe. He did a little repacking, made sure he had plenty of ammunition and, more important, a traveling bottle of Maryland rye whiskey. There was no telling what manner of horse piss would be passing for whiskey down in West Texas. Then he carried his gear out to the street and got a hackney.

"Denver and Rio Grande depot," he told the driver.

There were several rail lines serving Denver these days, each one of them going in a different direction. The funny thing was that he could have taken any one of them as a logical way to get to the Kiowa-Apache reservation. None of them was a *good* way to get there, of course, but any one of them would be just about as logical as the next. He settled for the D&RG because it would take him straight south as far as the Santa Fe neighborhood. From there he would have to find some other transportation.

The hack driver smiled at him. "Going on the excursion train, are you?"

"What?"

"You know. The special down to Lake Palmer. Mighty nice day for it is what I say, friend. Not so dang hot there. Bathe in the waters or just set and admire the young ladies." The man gave Longarm a knowing wink.

"I wish it was so," Longarm said. "Business."

"Oh." The driver sounded disappointed for him. Well, that was all right. Longarm felt disappointed for himself right now. There were things Custis Long would rather do than go down to the Pecos River country in the heat of summer and break a curse. He would, in fact, rather do almost anything than that.

Still, if the Bureau of Indian Affairs wanted him on loan from the Justice Department, they were going to have him. No question about that.

He settled back against the cracked leather of the hackney seat and thought about the problem the damned BIA had put in his lap.

After a while he gave it up with a sigh that probably would have gladdened Billy Vail's black heart. No sense in worrying about it until he got there and found out what the truth was about this stupidity. One thing was sure, though. Deputy Marshal Custis Long had scant faith in ghosties, goblins, or dark curses. If real people were really dying,

9

there was generally some real reason for it.

He sat back and enjoyed the ride after that. Time enough to worry when there was something to worry about.

The best rail connections he could get—and those were nothing to shout about—deposited him at Lamy, way the hell and gone southeast of Santa Fe. The rails went on down toward Albuquerque for a ways, but Longarm was hoping he could get a stage down the Pecos side of the mountain ranges and avoid having to cut across the Sacramentos. He had been in that country before, too, and it was even poorer than over on the Pecos side.

He was mildly regretful of having to leave the view inside the passenger coach. The woman across the aisle and one seat forward had a fine turn of ankle that she didn't mind showing. But much as he enjoyed a dalliance now and then, he wasn't going to start laying off the job for it. So he smoothed the bushy sweep of his moustache, gave the lady a secretive smile, and left the train at Lamy. Pity.

The town wasn't much except a stopover point for the rail cars, with a depot, a Harvey House, and a string of wagons and coaches that would transfer people up to the territorial capital for a suitable fee. Longarm deposited his gear at the railroad depot and hunted up the Overland Express agent.

"I need a stage down to . . ." Hell, it occurred to him that there wasn't a single major town or military post anywhere near the Kiowa-Apache reservation that he could point himself toward. There wasn't much down that way. "To Cottonwood, Texas," he finished lamely.

The express agent gave him a blank look.

"You know," Longarm prompted, "Cottonwood."

"Mister, I got coaches going to Sante Fe. I got coaches going to Santa Rosa. I ain't got nothing going to any part of Texas. Even if I'd heard of this Cottonwood place, which I ain't."

Half a block away, Longarm heard the hiss and clank and squeal of the train pulling out. He was beginning to think perhaps he should still be on it, but it was too late for that now.

"How about a freight haul, then? I'll take anything I can get."

The express agent shrugged. "You might find somebody hauling down to Lincoln. Or you might not. Hell, man, you might find some freighter that's going straight *to* this Cottonwood place. But if you want to count on that, why, I'd be real pleased to play you some cards just as soon as I can get this office closed. Which I would do right now on the spot if you're that much a fool."

This was not working out exactly the way it was supposed to.

"You say you have a coach as far as Santa Rosa. That's south, isn't it?"

The agent gave him a snooty, smug kind of look and said, "You have a fine grasp of geography, mister. Santa Rosa is south of here."

"Then I'll take a ticket for Santa Rosa on the earliest coach."

"Soon as you pay me eleven dollars and a half you'll take your ticket," the agent said.

Longarm was beginning to feel peeved with this fellow. He leaned over the counter until they were nose to nose. He was half a head taller than the Overland man and was solid muscle and rugged good looks, while the ticket taker worked indoors on his butt and looked it. Longarm reached up, making the officious little son of a bitch flinch, and gently straightened the man's tie for him. Then Longarm pulled out his wallet and displayed his badge. The major express companies still carried some mail despite the incursions of the railroads on that business, and they were expected to provide transportation to federal officers on official business.

The express agent gave Longarm a look that was no longer either snooty or smug. For a moment there he had been worried. For a moment there he had had reason to worry. "Sorry, sir. Let me get your ticket, sir."

"That would be real nice of you."

"Yes, sir." The man got a blank from a drawer under the counter, wrote on it, and stamped it with a flourish. "There you are, sir. Coach leaves in forty-five minutes. Just time enough for a meal if you want. Is there anything else you need, sir?"

"Not a thing, but thank you just the same."

"Yes, sir. Anything you need, you just speak up. And I'll make sure you don't miss the coach, Marshal."

Longarm felt a little ashamed of himself when he left the office. Not much, but a little. He turned toward the Harvey House. There was no telling when he might get another chance to eat or what the conditions might be when he did. The Harvey Houses that lined the railroads were never great, but they were dependable.

Nope, he thought as he walked toward the restaurant, *you just can't hardly get there from here.*

It was close to midnight when the Overland coach finally deposited him in Santa Rosa, and Longarm felt like hell. The train ride down to Lamy had been long and gritty. The coach ride to Santa Rosa had been long, gritty, and rough. Leather straps make poor springs, and a lightweight coach —likely there was no call for a bigger and more comfortable Concord on this nowhere route—can give a maverick mule a high run for its money when it comes to sheer bucking power.

"Last stop, ever'body out," the driver called out as he

brought the rig to a rocking halt in front of the express company's local office.

That was the extent of the enthusiasm for the arrival. The office was closed at this hour, and there was not even a hostler to help the driver unhitch and bed his team.

Longarm waited patiently while his fellow passengers groaned and crawled out of the coach. He had not exactly become friendly with any of them along the way. There was an aging man who was too deaf to hear when he was spoken to, and a plump woman with three toddling children gathered like so many chicks into the folds of her skirts. She had spent most of the trip giving Longarm looks of dark suspicion tinged with obvious fear of assault—rather completely unfounded—and the rest of her time in bitter complaint on those occasions when he reached for the comfort of a cheroot. The damned female was able to complain so loud and long that he had found it simpler to do without the smokes than to put up with her bitching. So his mood on arrival was about as low as his energy.

When the other passengers were gone—the old man shuffling off into the darkness and the woman and her brood being met by a man who, for no reason that Longarm could understand, seemed glad to see them—Longarm deposited his things on the sidewalk in front of the express office and gave the driver a hand with the four-up. The man accepted the help but gave no thanks in return.

But then, it had been that kind of trip.

"I don't suppose you could tell me where I might find a room for the night and a drink to settle the nerves," Longarm said.

The driver wordlessly pointed toward the far end of the town, where a few lights could still be seen. Everything else in or around Santa Rosa seemed to be closed for the night.

"Thanks," Longarm said sourly.

He hefted his carpetbag and saddle and carried them up the street.

There was only one hotel that he could see, and it did not look too promising. A lamp with the wick turned low was burning on the lobby counter, but the front door of the place was locked. That was close to being the last straw. Longarm banged on the glass and rattled the doorknob until a sleepy-eyed man in a nightshirt finally consented to come out and let him in.

"What do you want?" the fellow asked as he pulled the door open and rubbed a hand over the tangle of his hair.

Longarm's first inclination was to yell. What the hell would *anybody* want of a hotel in the middle of the damn night? No point in that, though. He bit his retort off and kept it behind his teeth. "I would like a room for the night," he said with exaggerated patience.

"Oh." The clerk stretched and shuddered and shambled over toward the desk, leaving Longarm to manage his own gear.

"Fifty cent," the man said. "An' you'll have to double up. We're kinda full."

Longarm hated having to share a room, but there were worse things possible after a day like this one. He paid his fee—trying to get somebody who was sound asleep to comprehend a government voucher was more than he wanted to take on right then—and signed the register.

"Room Fourteen. Second floor on the right."

Longarm took the key and hauled his things up the stairs. The door was relocked and the clerk out of sight before he reached the middle of the staircase.

There was one lamp kept burning in the hall. It was trimmed low, but it gave enough light for him to find the proper room and stumble into it.

He had been looking forward to a drink, but now that seemed like it would be an awful lot of trouble. Much too much trouble. Some other time.

There was no night lamp in the room, of course, so he struck a match to get an idea of the layout, which was spartan, and put his carpetbag on top of the bureau so he could get to the bottle of Maryland rye he was carrying. He took a pull on the jug and enjoyed the sensation of warmth that filled his belly. Some things a fellow could count on. With a huge, jaw-stretching yawn he kicked his stovepipe boots off and shed his tweed coat and vest and corduroy britches. He couldn't remember where the chair was, if there was a chair in the place, and certainly there was nothing as fancy in this room as a wardrobe, so he folded his outer clothing and placed it neatly on the floor with his snuff-brown Stetson on top.

His bedmate for the night was snoring lightly. Not loud enough to be bothersome, though. The man snorted a bit when Longarm sat on the side of the bed. The soft snoring stopped. Longarm sat still for a moment, and the sound resumed.

Gratefully Longarm slid under the blanket and allowed himself to relax. Lord, but he was tired. He thought he had time enough to get his eyes shut before he went to sleep himself, but he was so far gone that he really wasn't sure if it took him that long or not.

"Aw . . . *shit!*" Longarm sat up and looked with some disbelief at the scene in the small hotel room.

His carpetbag was standing open on the bureau. He was positive he had closed it last night. His hat was kicked off into a corner, his coat lying in a crumpled heap, although he had folded everything carefully before he laid it down.

And his damned bedmate was gone. Cleared out completely. How the man had managed to get out of the bed and rifle Longarm's gear and slip out of the room without waking him—well, he had damn sure been tired. More so than he had realized.

"Shit," he repeated.

He got up and checked to see what was missing. Most of his cash was safe. He had hidden that well enough. But his badge was gone, along with the wallet he carried it in. Probably the son of a bitch had thought he was getting Longarm's wad of cash when he found the wallet and he felt the lumpy badge inside it.

His telegraph key was gone. The thief would figure he could sell that obviously expensive instrument to somebody. Although what kind of market there could be for stray telegrapher's keys . . . "Shit."

The Winchester carbine was missing from the scabbard attached to his saddle.

His folded sheaf of government payment vouchers was gone. Hell, with the badge too the bastard could have a fine old time with those, and Uncle Sam would have to pay for whatever damage he did.

The bottle of Maryland rye was missing too.

"Son of a bitch," Longarm groaned.

He dressed in a hurry and strapped on his gunbelt.

A look out the window showed that it was past dawn, but not by much. Still and all, the miserable thief must have been out and away for some time already. A man always sleeps his deepest not long after he falls asleep. The bastard must have made his move not too long after Longarm got into bed.

Longarm carried his saddle and bag downstairs with him. He damn sure wasn't going to leave them in the room and have somebody else take a shot at them while he was away. He barged through the door the hotel clerk had come out of last night.

The man's quarters consisted of a small room directly off the back of the lobby. As Longarm could plainly see, the fellow didn't have much more in the way of comforts than the hotel guests received. But he did have company. And he was awake already. Not ready to get up, certainly, but awake. When Longarm walked in unannounced the clerk was screwing a skinny, dark-complected, bored-looking girl.

"What the hell . . . ?" the clerk yelped.

The girl—she might have been Mexican or Italian or even part Indian—looked at the tall, exceptionally handsome man who had just burst in on them, and smiled. The clerk rolled off her, exposing both of them to the waist. She did not seem to mind.

"I've been robbed," Longarm said.

"So go tell the town marshal about it. Now get the hell out of here."

"I'm leaving my bag and saddle behind your desk," Longarm said. "It's in your best interests to see that they're there when I get back."

"Yeah. Whatever." The clerk did not sound particularly distressed.

"Shit," Longarm mumbled as he left the room and pulled the door closed behind him. The skinny girl gave him a wistful look as he left.

Santa Rosa's town marshal had an office and jail across the street and a block down from the hotel. The place was unlocked but also unoccupied. Longarm managed to track the marshal down at a cafe next door to the hotel.

He introduced himself and told Marshal Sam Yorick what his problem was.

Yorick was a large, slow-moving, slow-talking man who continued to eat while Longarm talked. The man was stuffing himself with fried mush drowned in syrup. It did nothing to pique Longarm's appetite.

"Are you listening to me?" Longarm asked at one point.

"Ayuh," Yorick said around a mouthful of the gooey yellow stuff.

"I need the stage line checked to see if anybody left town that way. And the livery, wherever that is. I need to make sure nobody leaves this damn place before that bastard can get away with federal identification. And those government vouchers. That is a federal crime, you know."

"Need a lot, don't ya, son," Yorick said gently. He was probably in his fifties and looked as though he had not moved at any pace faster than dead slow in twenty years.

"Now, look, damn it, we are talking about federal offenses here. The Justice Department—"

"Calm down." Yorick raised another forkful of mush to his mouth, smacked his lips, and shoved it in. He seemed to be enjoying it regardless of how revolting Longarm thought it looked.

"But, damn it, man, I have to—"

"You do what you want, son, but what I suggest is you calm down." Yorick chewed slowly on the mush.

Feeling quite thoroughly exasperated, Longarm slammed a palm on the table in frustration and turned away.

"Whoa," Yorick said gently.

Longarm whirled back to face him. "What?" he snapped.

"What'd you say your name was, son?" The marshal actually took enough interest to lay his fork down.

"Long," Longarm snapped. "Custis Long. Deputy U.S. marshal out of the Denver District, United States Justice Department, William Vail, marshal."

"Uh-huh." Yorick picked up his fork again and rearranged the few slices of mush still on his sticky plate. "Long way from home, aren't you?"

"Special assignment to the Department of the Interior," Longarm said peevishly.

"Uh-huh." Yorick took one more bite, wiped his lips thoughtfully, and dropped his napkin onto the plate.

"Are you going to—"

"No need to get yourself so worked up," Yorick said slowly. "You say you're missing a Winchester carbine?"

"Is there a point to all this time-wasting?"

"I certainly think so," Yorick said calmly.

18

"I am missing a Winchester carbine," Longarm said with a show of long-suffering patience.

"Wouldn't happen to recall the serial number of that weapon, would you?"

"As a matter of fact, I do." Longarm repeated it for him.

"Uh-huh." Yorick pulled out an oversized pipe and began to load it. "Don't mind if I have a smoke, do you, son?"

"What does that have to do with—"

"I'll assume you don't mind," Yorick said. He struck a match and took his time about getting the pipe lighted, moving the flame slowly back and forth across the surface of the carefully tamped tobacco until he was completely satisfied.

"Jesus," Longarm groaned.

Yorick smiled at him. "Exactly."

"What?"

"Looks after damn fools like you and me." The marshal puffed slowly on his pipe.

"But what . . . ?"

"In this business of peace officering, son, it's nice to be good. Better, though, t' be lucky." The pipe sizzled a little, and Yorick frowned. "Humph. Must have got too much moisture in that humidor. I'll have to do something about that."

Longarm rolled his eyes and would have turned again to leave, but Yorick stopped him with a touch on the wrist. "I kinda wanted to make sure the stuff you say was stolen from you was really stolen from you. A stranger, now, might know the name of a passin' Yew Ess of Ay deputy. Wouldn't be so likely to know the serial number of a deputy's carbine, would he?"

"What the hell does that have to do with anything?"

"Like I said, luck is handy when you have it."

"But . . ."

"Your things are over to my office, son."

"What?"

Yorick smiled and puffed on his pipe. "I might point out to you, son, that you came in here hostile, blood in your eye, all set to tell this poor ole local fool what needed to be done, and full of yourself. Fact is, son, not every local fool is a complete fool. Which is something you might want to keep in mind, time to time." Yorick's smile was gentle. "An' some of us do get lucky now and then. Fact is, I picked up your friend last night. Dog sick and stone drunk. I got your things *and* your drunk at the jail. Everything except that bottle of whiskey. He finished that off, mostly. Fell down and broke the bottle, so what he didn't drink was spilt."

Longarm started to snap at the Santa Rosa marshal. Then he paused for a moment and shook his head. "You know, of course, that I feel like nine kinds of a fool myself right now."

"That's all right, son. I been lawing for better than thirty years now, and I still forget to take folks serious now and then. But I'm tryin' to get over it. Hard thing to remember sometimes."

Longarm found himself grinning. "Yes, sir."

"Buy you some breakfast son, before we go over an' collect your possessions?"

Longarm chuckled. "Marshal Yorick, I'd be proud to have breakfast with you."

"Now I'm pleased to hear you say that, son, because I haven't got my fill of coffee yet this morning. And I'm just not worth a damn until I get my coffee." Yorick turned and motioned for the waiter, and Longarm pulled out a chair at the slow-talking local fool's table.

It surely was true that a man could learn things when he least expected to.

Chapter 3

There was a local short-haul stage connection down to Lincoln, but with transportation so poorly organized in this wide-open and barely populated country Longarm decided instead to hitch a ride with a freighter down to Fort Sumner where there was a skeleton garrison and a Remount Service buying point.

He did not care one way or the other about the handful of infantry troops still manning the post, but a Remount horse was going to be indispensable.

Longarm had his pick from sixty-odd head of typical Remount Service animals, each of them a uniform 15-2, give or take a finger, and each of them bay to brown in color. There was never anything fancy about a Remount horse, but the beasts were generally hell for tough.

"We haven't put these through combat training," a graying first lieutenant told him, "so I can't promise they'll stand calm in the face of gunfire. Might or might not, so I make you no promises." Before the animals were turned over to the army for issue, each horse would have to prove itself by way of a training program that in many ways was more exhaustive—and more thorough—than that given to the troopers who would ride them.

"Thanks for the tip," Longarm told him, "but if I get lucky for the rest of this job he won't have to hear any loud noises."

The particular horse Longarm took was a seal brown, drab of color but deep in the chest and with well developed muscle. A few minutes with the old McClellan on his back and Longarm knew that whoever had broken this one had done a good job of it. The animal had a look that shouted stamina and was quick-footed enough to work cattle, with an easy way of going that would be a damn sight better than the rattle and shake of a stagecoach.

"Where are you bound?" the officer asked. "If you don't mind the question, that is."

"It's no secret." Longarm told him.

"Empty country down there," the officer said. "I used to chase Comanche out of Davis and later on Apache too. They're most cleaned out of there now, which is why there are some folks moving in, but that country used to be hell. Practically no surface water, though you can dig in the dry beds and find some if you have the time for that. Rough country to chase hostiles through, let me tell you."

"Do you know this Cottonwood place?"

"If it's the one I'm thinking of, I do. Used to be called San Felipe de Avila, but that was a while black."

"How'd it come to have an Anglo name now?"

The lieutenant shrugged. "Apaches, mostly. The Mexicans that used to live there survived the Comanch', but the Apaches came east one raid and just about wiped them out. Killed every adult they could find and carried off the young ones. Burnt what they could and tore down what wouldn't burn. I remember that raid. I lost three good troopers who

22

were off on a water detail and never once laid eyes on a live Apache. But that was a while ago. What Apache are left off the reservation are down in Mexico now. We haven't had a real raid this far east in, oh, I don't know how long."

"What about these Kiowa-Apache? Know anything about them?"

"Everything I need to know," the lieutenant said bitterly. "You know what they say. If he's breathing he ain't a good Indian. 'Specially Apache. Mean sons of bitches, the Apache."

"These are Kiowa-Apache," Longarm said. He had his own opinions about this dead Indian/good Indian business, but he was not going to argue the point with this end-of-career Remount man.

"Makes no difference. If you say Apache, you've already said son of a bitch. That's the way I see it."

"Well, thank you for your help." Longarm secured his carpetbag behind the cantle of the McClellan, checked again to make sure his Spanish bit was fitted properly to the horse's mouth, and swung into the saddle.

"Any time, Marshal. We're here to serve. If you're going to old San Felipe, just follow the Pecos down till you see Guadalupe Peak off to the west and turn toward it. There's a seasonal creek there, likely dry this time of year. San Felipe de Avila is on the south side of the creekbed. You can't miss it."

"Much obliged." Longarm touched the brim of his Stetson in farewell and turned the leggy brown to the south, away from the dry, sun-baked compound of Fort Sumner and down the Pecos.

With officers like that one in the country he was hoping that he would not have to call on the army for assistance if things were sticky down at the Kiowa-Apache reservation.

For that matter, it would be nice if the civilians around Cottonwood, Texas, had not adopted those same bloody views. Longarm had scant expectations for that kind of good luck, though. Not the way this job had started out, he didn't.

It was not a difficult journey from Fort Sumner to Cottonwood, but it was tedious. Five days on horseback. He could have made it in four, but that would have been pushing the horse's stamina. A man became used to rapid transportation when he lived near a hub of railroad activity, Longarm reflected as he rode. Five days by rail would get a man halfway across the continent.

He was following the Pecos River all the way, so water was not a problem. The water in the Pecos was sluggish and slightly alkaline but palatable. Elsewhere in this country he was covering, water could be very much of a problem.

Each day he rode through innumerable creekbeds and washes, but at this time of year very nearly all of them were dry as a lizard's belly. Come a melt after snowfall in the low string of mountains off to the west—or at any time of year after a rainstorm somewhere on higher ground— the Pecos and any of its tributaries could become a rip-snorting son of a bitch. But not now.

The farther south he rode, the drier and more barren the land became as well.

Off to the east on the other side of the Pecos the Llano Estacado, the famed Staked Plains, lay flat as a dinner table and just about as brushy as a planed and polished tabletop too. A little grass grew there, but not much.

To the west, toward the meager humps that these Southwesterners called mountains—damned near insulting for a Colorado man who grew up in West Virginia to hear that tag tied to a mound of bare rock—the Sacramentos and Guadalupes snagged a bit of moisture out of the sky from time to time and seeped it down so that some grass and mesquite would grow. In and along the dry washes there were even a few straggly cottonwoods.

Even on the plain that rose from the river toward the mountains, though, the grasses were sparse and short and brown. A cow could make a living off them, Longarm saw, but she would have to cover some territory to get her gut full. He stopped early of an evening and hobbled the brown horse so it would be able to forage wide enough to get itself a feeding. More trouble come the morning saddling when he had to walk out and catch the animal but more sensible than gaunting a good horse. He had chosen the horse because it looked stout. If he had wanted a poor one there were several he might have picked that were already in that state.

People were even more rare in this country than shade trees. After his first day Longarm saw damned few folks. A talkative man in this country could have his voice box atrophy and wither away from disuse.

The second day he saw a flock of sheep off to the west. There must have been a herder with them, but if so the fellow was not announcing himself. Longarm saw nothing identifiably human but had to figure he was being watched.

On the afternoon of the third day he rode up to the lip of yet another dry streambed—it could have been the some-time-running Rio Penasco—and surprised both himself and a group of cowboys who were watering a band of horses in the Pecos.

There were four young men in the human herd, probably thirty-odd head of coarse-bred ponies in the four-legged bunch. The horses were too tired and thirsty to respond much to a horse and rider showing up on the bank above them, but the boys looked edgy.

"Howdy," Longarm said. By then it sounded strange to hear a word in the air. He had not spoken to anyone since he said goodbye to the lieutenant back at Sumner.

25

"Howdy yourself," the nearest of the cowboys said.

"Hot day." Longarm pulled a kerchief from his pocket and used it to wipe his face. It wasn't so much that he wanted to wipe his face as that he wanted to show these fellows that he was willing to take his hand away from the butt of the Colt that was riding in a cross-draw holster at his waist.

"Sure hell is." The youngster reached up and scratched his nose, probably for very much the same reason.

"I was fixing to stop and boil myself some coffee," Longarm lied. "I could make enough for five."

"Neighborly of you, but . . ."

"I'd enjoy some," another of the riders cut in. He was the smallest of the bunch, buck-toothed and with a small, pinched-looking face. He was probably the youngest of them too although likely none of them had seen twenty-five yet.

The first youngster gave him a look that said he didn't agree but gave in. He pointed west and said, "There's an easy slope down off that rim a couple hundred yards back."

"All right." Longarm turned the brown that way. The slope was gentle enough right where he was that the horse could have made it without too much sliding, but if they wanted a word in private they were welcome to it.

He found the indicated spot, dropped down into the wash, and rode back through the deep, soft sand.

Thirty-two head of loose horses, he noted as he returned. The boys were all riding tough little barbs with short backs and skinny little legs that could go damn near forever before they played out. The loose horses were poorer bred and poorly kept, with burrs in their forelocks and tails that had never been trimmed. Real brush-tail scrubs, but gentled enough to handle.

He couldn't help but notice, too, that three of the boys were riding horses branded C Lazy T and the fourth one a VII, which might have read Roman Seven. All the loose

26

stock was jaw-branded with a small P. Not that the differences were necessarily significant.

One of the boys had a fire put together and beginning to burn by the time Longarm got back to them, and they had all loosened their cinches. Prepared to be friendly, Longarm concluded. He was willing to do the same.

Longarm got out his coffee pot and paper twist of Arbuckle's, then slipped the cinch under his McClellan and put the hobbles on the brown so it could drink or graze if it wished. Behind him one of the boys was unwrapping a bloody hunk of meat from a cloth.

"You have a taste for lamb?" the buck-toothed kid asked.

"After eating my own cooking for the past couple days I'd have a taste for lamb berries if there was a good sauce to put over 'em." The reference was to sheep shit, which comes out in pellets much like those of a rabbit or a deer. The four boys chuckled, and one of them began to slice strips off the piece of meat while another one fetched out a skillet and rubbed some bacon in it for the grease.

"Where you bound from if you don't mind me asking?" the youngest one asked.

"North," Longarm said. "Headed south." Custom and habit prevented him from being too specific about his origin or destination.

He thought the boys passed some glances around among themselves.

"We're crossing," one of them said, not bothering to say whether they were headed east or west. Not that he had to. The tracks their horses had left showed that they had already crossed the river from the east before they stopped to water the animals and take a break. It was the sort of caution a man on the run might take if he thought there might be pursuit coming along behind him.

On the other hand, it was also the sort of thing a prudent drover would do to make sure he was not caught on the wrong side of a river in case a flash flood came up. Just because the sun was shining over him did not mean that a storm fifty miles away and a nighttime back was already sending a wall of water down toward him.

"Poor time of year to be on the Llano," Longarm said.

"Ain't that the truth."

"Hell, mister, there *ain't* no good time of year on the Llano."

"Never could figure why the Comanche wanted to keep that country so bad. I sure hell wouldn't fight anybody for it."

The coffee was ready by the time the meat was, and they shared what was available.

When he was done Longarm stood, intending to take his pot down to the river and rinse the coffee grounds out of it. He had an itch on his belly and went to scratch it. When his hand moved in the direction of his belt buckle—and in the direction as well of the holstered Colt—all four boys suddenly tensed. One of them grabbed toward his gun.

Longarm grinned at them and scratched, sighing out loud at the relief that gave him.

Three of the boys laughed a bit. The one who had reached for his gun coughed and held his side like he had developed a sudden hitch there.

Very slowly Longarm picked up the pot. "Anybody want the last of this before I clean it out?"

"I'll take it," the buck-toothed kid said. He held his cup out and Longarm poured what little was left, most of that grounds. The kid did not seem to mind.

"Thanks."

"Any time."

Longarm caught his horse, replaced the pot in his saddlebag, and led the animal back near the fire. "I thank you for the meal and the company."

"Any time, neighbor."

He tightened his cinch and mounted. "Good luck to

28

you." With a touch of his hatbrim he kneed the brown into motion and rode south again, leaving the four cowboys and their herd of horses behind.

An empty, lonesome country, he thought. But not so empty or so lonesome that a man couldn't get himself shot dead in it if he was proddy or just wanted to be a damn fool.

Off to the west the sun was starting to sink down toward the tops of the Guadalupes. The reservation would be somewhere off in that direction, and not too far away the Cottonwood residents who thought the Kiowa-Apache had put a curse on them. Longarm wondered what kind of damn fools he would find at Cottonwood.

Chapter 4

Cottonwood wasn't much.

Longarm approached it from the east, following the dry, sandy creekbed up from the Pecos the way the lieutenant had suggested. The town lay in a bend in the sometime river, with the flat expanse of sand curving along the entire south side of the town and a stand of cottonwood trees between the town and the dry bed. Out in what would sometimes be the stream channel there was a hump of land, an island of sorts, that also had some cottonwood and crackwillow growth on it.

Between the island and the bank someone or something had carved a depression into the bed, trapping a pool of stagnant water when the flow receded. The pool was low now and thick with green scum, but it probably was handy for watering town stock like horses and mules for much of the year.

Obviously there was a good supply of underground

water inside the bend of the streambed, because just about every house and business Longarm could see had its own well dug close by to it.

The buildings were weather-grayed frame affairs for the most part, a few of them made from cheaper and cooler and locally produced adobe.

The Remount officer had said the place used to be a Mexican town before the Texans took it over, but there was little sign of that now. The adobe buildings that were in use now were newly built, or relatively so. Sun-baked mud bricks tend to melt and sag with age, and the corners of an old 'dobe are never tidily square, but rounded off with age and weathering. All of the adobes that showed any hint of life at all now were still pretty much plumb.

Here and there Longarm could see some low adobe walls that showed weathering, and on the far side of the town there were some tumbledown ruins, roofless half-walls, that might once have been a church or mission or some other public building when the place was still called San Felipe de Ávila.

Except for that, though, it would have been difficult to guess that Cottonwood used to be a Mexican village.

Now it looked pretty much like any other small Texas town, with a few stores and a few houses and more attention paid to water and to livestock than to the people who lived here.

The transportation Longarm could see on the main street of the town was mostly in the form of saddle horses, with a few small utility wagons and a complete absence of fancy driving rigs. The amenities of high society hadn't reached Cottonwood yet.

That was about enough mulling and delay, Longarm told himself. Time to get to work. He lighted a cheroot and headed into town.

There was no jail and no city hall that he could see. Likely the people of Cottonwood had not yet gotten to that

31

point either. He settled for the nearest of several saloons in sight on the assumption that he could find a free lunch counter and some information there. He tied the brown to the rail outside the place and retrieved the coat he had been carrying rolled up behind his cantle.

While he was doing that a man came out of the fly-bead curtained doorway and stopped to watch him. A stranger was in town. That would be big news in a place like this.

"Howdy," Longarm said easily.

The man did not answer, just continued to stand and inspect him.

"Something bothering you, mister?" Longarm asked.

The man turned his eyes from Longarm's gear—the hornless McClellan would be an oddity in cattle country like this—and briefly met Longarm's glance. Then, still without speaking, the fellow turned away and hurried off toward the next block of storefronts. Longarm shrugged and went inside the saloon.

The place was no great shakes, but its shade was more than welcome. The relative darkness gave a false impression of being cool inside. Hot as it was in the sun, false was close enough.

A few drinkers were at the bar, and two men were playing rummy at one of the tables. Even the bartender looked bored. When Longarm came in, everyone stopped what they were doing—if loafing could be considered to be doing anything—and turned to stare.

"Afternoon, gentlemen," Longarm said. He went to the bar, and the bar-keep almost reluctantly came down the other side of it to serve him.

"Beer," he said. "And if you have any Maryland rye, I'd take a fresh bottle of that too." Ever since Santa Rosa Longarm had been missing the bottle that sorry little bastard of a thief had gone and broken.

The barkeep served him the beer and collected a nickel.

"Got no rye here," he said. "I got some trade whiskey if you want that."

"Not hardly." There was no telling what might be thrown into a batch of trade whiskey. Water taken from a tank where cattle pissed would be the best of the brew. That and cheap alcohol and whatever else came to hand, including gunpowder and slightly used plugs of chewing tobacco.

"Mostly we drink beer around here."

"It will do," Longarm said.

Beer was a sensible enough drink in this climate. A man sweated so damn much that he was always needing more fluids in his system. Besides, it was hard to foul a keg of beer once the brewery plugged it.

One of the drinkers at the bar a few feet away sidled closer and dragged his beer along with him.

Longarm raised his sudsy mug in the fellow's direction, then drank.

The man nodded. It was the warmest reception Longarm had yet seen in Cottonwood.

"Passing through?" the man asked.

"Not really." Longarm took another pull on his beer and ground the stub of his cheroot out under his boot sole.

The man grunted wordlessly and took another long, hard look at this stranger.

"You'd be the federal man," the fellow said. He did not make it sound like much of a question, more a statement of fact.

"That's so," Longarm admitted. "But how would you know about that?"

Instead of answering the man bent over the bar, looking down into his mug. "We don't need no federal men around here."

"That isn't the way I heard . . ."

There was a faint rattle of wooden beads from the doorway, and Longarm turned to see two tall, exceptionally lean men push through the fly curtain. "You heard the gentleman," the first through said. "We don't need federal help here."

"And who would you be?" Longarm asked.

He took a look at the two. They were alike enough to have been baked in the same mold. Same strung-out frames. Same slightly undershot jaws. Same pale eyes. Same lank ends of dirty blond hair sticking down from under the sweat-caked bands of tall, uncreased hats. About the only difference Longarm could see between them was that one was wrinkled by age and weather both, the other wrinkled only slightly and that all by weather. The older one was probably in his forties, the younger likely still in his late teens. Father and son, Longarm guessed. They almost had to be.

By way of answer the older one pulled his vest back to expose a badge pinned to his shirt just under the top left edge of the vest.

Both of them came to the bar, and the man who had just been so curious moved aside to make room for them.

"My information was that there wasn't any law in Cottonwood yet."

"There's a law in Texas, mister," the older one said.

"Rangers?"

"Ranger. The boy ain't old enough yet to draw the pay. Old enough to earn it, though. Older'n I was when I first joined." The father sounded proud of the son who was following him into the family business.

"I see," Longarm said. He introduced himself.

The Ranger was Ned Sharply. The boy was known as Junior. It certainly fit.

"Long, eh?" Sharply said. "Call you Longarm, don't they?"

"That's right."

"They coulda sent worse, I reckon."

Longarm assumed he was supposed to take that as a compliment.

"But we ain't needing help," Sharply added.

"That wasn't the way I heard it, Ned. I heard some people have died down here."

Sharply nodded. "Four of 'em. Soon be five."

Longarm raised an eyebrow.

"Four folks has died, two of 'em younguns. There's another child took sick. She'll die 'fore the week is out sure as day follows night."

"From a curse," Longarm said.

Sharply shrugged. "Not my business to say why they're dead. Dead is dead, Deputy. No denyin' that. Dead is dead."

"When people take sick and die, Ned, it generally isn't a matter for the law."

"Is in this case," Sharply said. "Everybody knows what's killin' 'em. It's those stinkin' Injuns. Injuns killin' white folks, that makes it a matter for the law."

"Damn right, Papa," Junior said.

"What makes you think it's the Indians causing it?" Longarm asked.

Sharply did not answer. Probably the Ranger did not want to say anything out loud that could be taken for foolishness by those who failed to accept curses and witches and haunts as reality, but his son was not so circumspect.

"Everybody knows it," Junior said. "Everybody seen the curse put on. The stinkin' damn Injuns did it right in plain sight. Put them a curse on this town an' not three weeks later folks started taking sick an' now dyin'."

"That's neither here nor there," the elder Sharply said, apparently wanting to change the subject. "Point is, Deputy, we got things in hand. This soil is part o' the sov'reign state o' Texas. I am a duly constituted an' commissioned officer representin' said sov'reign state. We can handle it. Don't need you. Don't want you."

35

"You Rangers taking charge of federal matters too these days?"

"I already told you, this here is Texas, an'—"

"The Kiowa-Apache reservation is federal land, under federal jurisdiction. My jurisdiction, that is. And everything off the reservation just a few miles north of here is in New Mexico Territory. The territorial government is under federal management. And come to that, why, Texas is part of the U.S. these days. Or hadn't you heard?"

Sharply gave him a cold look. "I did hear somethin' about that."

"But you didn't like it?"

"That's right. I didn't like it."

"We don't have to be at odds on this thing," Longarm said mildly. "I don't see any reason why a Texas Ranger and a federal deputy can't work together."

"I do," Ned Sharply said.

Both Sharplys turned, the son following so quickly that it looked like one single motion to turn the two of them, and walked out of the saloon.

"You might ought to pay attention to what Ned says, mister," the bartender said. "Ned and his boy are the law here now. We don't need you."

Longarm smiled and winked at the man. "But you got me, friend. You sure hell got me now."

He drained off the last of his beer and left to see if he could find a more congenial place in Cottonwood.

If there was a congenial place in Cottonwood, Texas, Custis Long couldn't find it.

There was no hotel in the town at all, much less a good one. But then this was not the sort of place where visitors came to take the waters. Would not have been even if folks could find any waters to take. This was the sort of place where people came to work and try to wrest some sort of living from the dry grasses and the hard-baked soil. The sheep and cattle raised in the vicinity would have to be herded out to the railroad, so there would not even be stock buyers coming here as transients.

If anyone in Cottonwood was willing to rent out rooms to boarders they were being secretive about it. Longarm could not even find a house willing to rent him space.

That was unusual, but eventually he got the message about it.

"I am truly sorry," a doe-eyed little woman told him. She was a young thing and probably had been pretty when she married, but young as she was that had been long enough ago to make a difference. Now she had one toddler hanging onto her skirts, a second one in a basket beside her washtub, and maybe five-ninths of the next pushing at the front of her dress. She already looked worn out, and there were dark circles under her pretty eyes. "Lord knows we could use the extra money, and there's space enough in the lean-to off the kitchen. But my man has been talking with those Sharplys, you see, and he nor any of his friends would be fit to live around if I was to let you come in here. I wish I could help you out, but . . ."

"I understand, ma'am. I certainly wouldn't want to cause you trouble."

"I'm glad you aren't angry, Marshal. Thank you."

"My place to thank you, ma'am, for being the only person in town decent enough to tell me to my face." Longarm squatted down and winked at the little one—he couldn't tell if it was a boy or a girl—who was peeking at him with one eye out of a fold in mama's skirt.

"That right there is the reason for it, Marshal," the child's mother said.

"Ma'am?"

She bent to gather the child into her arms and raise it to straddle her hip. She chucked him—the baby was wearing only a short shift and Longarm could see now that it was a boy—under the chin and said, "I was saying that this here is the reason we're all so worried. Be so glad when the problems with the Indians are over. Babies, Marshal. They tell me that Indians don't care much about babies. Think of them the way white folks would think of a puppy, Ranger Sharply says. But we think high of our young around here, Marshal. And you probably heard already that of the four people that's been killed, two have been children. And one a young mother."

"Yes, ma'am." Longarm playfully squeezed one of the little boy's dirty toes, and the child began to cry. "I'm sorry, ma'am, I was just . . ."

"I know, Marshal. He's just a mite shy with folks he doesn't know. We don't see so many around here that he's ever had the chance to get used to seeing strangers. Don't fret yourself about it." She held the child tight against her and bounced up and down on her toes to rock him into silence again.

"What you've heard about those Indians, ma'am . . ."

"It's the truth, Marshal. We've seen, you know. When we went out there and all seen them put the curse on us. We all of us saw how they ignore those poor red children. It was scandalous. And discipline? Why, you never saw such a pack of little animals. They were just let to run wild, Marshal. Like puppies. Just like Ranger Sharply said, though none of us had heard about that at the time, of course. But we saw it for ourselves, even before Ranger Sharply got here."

"I think what you saw, what you remember, is all a matter of interpretation, ma'am. But I've been wanting to ask someone about that . . . uh . . . curse you saw applied. What . . ."

Inside the house there was the hiss and bubble of a pot starting to boil over onto the stove, and the infant in the basket chose that moment to wake up with an impatient shriek.

Almost quicker than Deputy Long could get his gun out,

the little housewife had the older boy down on his feet, the younger child in her arms, and was racing inside to get the boiling pot off the fire.

Longarm shook his head. He doubted she would believe him anyway, even if he did get her to listen to him about Indian notions of child-rearing.

But puppies? Lack of affection? Lordy, these folks actually believed that.

There wasn't much that could be any further from the truth than a belief like that, but how do you go and convince someone of the truth when they have generations of hatred and fear to fuel misunderstandings that they will almost willfully cling to?

Not that there was any point in trying right now.

Longarm turned away from the porch and gave up his search for lodgings in Cottonwood. At least he knew now that that would be a waste of time.

And no harm done, of course. He had slept without a roof once or twice in the past. He supposed he could survive for another night or two on his own.

He ignored the rest of the residences in town and went to the general mercantile. He would be wanting a few extra things if he was going to be bedding in a camp, particularly a dry one. He would want to buy a couple of extra canteens. He always carried one slab-sided, blanket-covered canteen with him, but in this arid country he might have to carry water for the horse too.

He was thinking as he walked, planning what he should get and what he might not need here that he would have required in the higher, colder country to the north.

There were two general stores in Cottonwood but no greengrocer. There would not be enough surface water for garden irrigation on any great scale, and the town was much too far from anything else for fresh produce to be shipped in. Probably everything except fresh meat and a little milk would have to be brought in canned or dried, or simply left out of the diet. It would make for a lifetime of plain fare.

Longarm bought his canteens and a collapsible canvas bucket to water the horse from. He laid in some supplies of tinned and dried foods, much more than he would have asked the horse to carry on an extended trip, but not so much of a burden on a short ride to establish a camp in the vicinity.

While he was paying for his purchases he noticed the shelves behind the merchant's counter.

"You carry plenty of shotshells," he mentioned.

"Yeah. Plenty good bird shooting around here. The white-wings come to the ponds every night, you know. Fine shooting and even better eating."

"I got to agree with that," Longarm said. "Broiled dove breast is about as good eating as anything can be."

The storekeeper nodded. "Not so many birds this year as there used to be, though. That's why I still got so many shells on hand. Ordered in cases of the things, an' I still got most of them to sell." He shrugged. "They'll be strong again next year, I reckon."

"Sure." Longarm took another look toward an empty section on the end of the shelf. "Looks like you're shy on .44-40s, though."

The storekeeper grunted. "Winchester .44-40s, Colt .45s, Smith an' Wesson .44s, even the old rimfire .44s. I'm near cleaned out on those. Got another shipment due in on the next freight, though, if you need some."

"I have enough for right now, thanks. You had a run on sales, did you?"

The storekeeper seemed to remember now who it was he was talking to. He got a nervous, half-embarrassed look about him and glanced toward the door as if to see if anyone was listening. "Nothing like that, Marshal. No, sirree.

Nothing like that. I just got behind on my ordering. That's all."

"I see. Well, I thank you." Longarm picked up his change and left the place.

This was damned interesting. A run on the sales of centerfire cartridges. The storekeeper might want to deny that, but it seemed plain that that was what had happened.

There were not a whole hell of a lot of reasons why an entire community would be concerned about arming itself.

Longarm could not think of a single one of those possible reasons that would please him.

He was beginning to think he had better make some sense out of this curse nonsense before Texas went to war with the Kiowa-Apache nation. *And* with the federal government, as administrators of the rights of that nation.

Lordy, Longarm told himself as he headed toward his horse. How do you break a curse? Particularly one you don't believe in to begin with?

That could be a bit of a problem.

Chapter 5

It was too late in the day to head for the reservation, which was a good twenty miles out of town, and too early for turning in. Besides, Longarm was hungry, and he could see no point in cooking for himself when there were perfectly good—or at least perfectly available—cafes in Cotton-wood. He had seen two of them in town, and nearly anything would be better than a supper taken out of a can.

There was no livery in Cottonwood, but there was a sale barn where someone had set up business as a horse buyer —a sign over the sagging door gave him that information —but must have failed. The place was abandoned now and in poor repair. Still, it had a corral and the better part of a roof. Longarm put the brown in the corral and unsaddled it, piling his gear inside what was left of the barn. The failed sale barn was out near the ruins of the adobe church.

At first look he had thought the old church was the last remnant of San Felipe de Avila, but when he was looking for a room he had noticed that a good many of the houses built and occupied by the Texans had beehive ovens built of old adobe behind them. So apparently San Felipe de Avila had been a town of fair size in its day.

He made sure the horse had water in a trough made from an ancient cottonwood trunk section, then walked back into town.

At this time of evening the local men whose work was close enough to permit them their evenings in town had begun to ride in, and there was a great deal more activity on the street than there had been.

Word about the presence of a federal deputy must have spread. Certainly everyone acted like they knew who he was and what his business here was. Yet he noticed that no one was openly unpleasant. They simply kept their distance. Sharply's influence did not condone rebellion in any form. Just an attitude that Longarm's mission here was an unwanted annoyance. These people pretty obviously intended to take care of their problems themselves.

It had, after all, been the Bureau of Indian Affairs that asked him in on the case, not the town of Cottonwood. Longarm wondered if the agent out at the reservation could help him get a handle on this curse nonsense.

But that would have to wait until tomorrow. Right now it was getting late, and he was hungry.

He turned in at the first cafe he came to. The place was small but busy. It had a number of small, individual tables, most of which were full. There were several women among the customers, most of them young, and some children as well. Cottonwood itself was a young town, and apparently it was populated with young, strong families intent on carving a life for themselves out of a raw, arid land.

There was no empty table in the cafe, so Longarm pulled out a chair at a table already half occupied by two men who looked like they had spent the day in their saddles. "Room for one more, gentlemen?"

43

One of them shrugged and looked away. The other glanced toward his companion first, then said, "Room for four."

Both men got up, tipped their hats forward, and left the place. They had only been there long enough to get their coffee but had not yet eaten.

The tables were being waited by a girl, probably still in her teens, and Longarm would have guessed probably also the daughter of the cook who could be seen at the stove at the back of the one-room place. The girl watched her two customers leave, then came to the table without comment.

"I'm sorry," Longarm said. "I surely didn't mean to drive any of your trade away."

The girl said nothing, just stood waiting for his order.

Longarm looked around the room. No one else in the place was talking now, although there had been a low, pleasant buzz of conversation when he came inside it. Now the diners were eating in silence, concentrating on their plates and looking nowhere but down.

No one in Cottonwood was being rude to him. Not exactly. If he wished to make a purchase he was welcome to do so. If he wanted to order a meal they would serve him.

If he wanted conversation or pleasant company he would have to go elsewhere.

"I guess I'm not that hungry after all," he said. He laid down the napkin he had picked up and shoved his chair back from the table.

Still no one said anything. No one looked toward him. The girl stood waiting patiently for him to order or to leave.

Longarm left the cafe, went back to his horse, and left Cottonwood, Texas.

He was half a mile out of town before he realized that he still had not replaced the bottle that had been stolen from him in Santa Rosa. He had intended to do that in Cottonwood. He would be damned, though, if he was going to ride back for that. The whole damn town would have been watching him ride out. He was not going to turn around and go back now. He checked his pockets. Thank goodness he had a decent enough supply of cheroots.

But tonight's was going to be a more lonesome camp than usual. It was not that he minded his own company. Lord knew, he got enough of that and never minded it when he was on the trail somewhere and had to make a camp for one. He never minded that. It was just the idea that back in Cottonwood people would be drinking and eating and talking. Talking to that Ranger, for one thing, and listening to what Ned Sharply had to say about Indians and Indian children and probably how to fight Indians too.

Damn that Sharply, Longarm thought. This job probably wouldn't be half so unpleasant if it weren't for the Ranger.

Still, things would look brighter tomorrow. Maybe tomorrow he could even get some straight facts about what was going on here.

Longarm damn sure hoped so.

The trail from Cottonwood to the reservation's agency headquarters was clearly marked with wagon ruts. It led west along the route of the dry creekbed, then angled north as it neared the Guadalupes. From there it climbed sharply up in elevation and continued in a northwesterly direction.

Even though it climbed into what were locally called mountains—which would have been a pretty good joke if anyone had been joking about it—there was no noticeable improvement in the water table or the vegetation. If any-thing the sere, gray bluffs and knobs and escarpments were rawer, drier, and even more rugged than the relatively flat plain below.

This country was dry, dusty, gritty, and drab. Longarm had the uncharitable thought that maybe the Kiowa-Apache should join forces with the Texans and both sides argue that the tribe be moved to more hospitable ground. But then

Uncle Sam was not noted for giving away choice territory to his copper-colored wards.

The wall of mountains Longarm was climbing into was a jagged series of ledges, niches, and ancient waterways cut, gouged, and stabbed into gray rock.

A footpath cut uphill from the road at one point, and curiosity prompted him to pull the brown to a halt. He told himself that the horse was due for a rest anyway, although it was barely damp with sweat on its shoulders. He wanted to see where the path led.

The walk was only a hundred yards or so and brought him to a regular oasis. Or certainly what would pass for one until the real thing came along.

Set in the middle of all the gray dryness was a gravel-bottomed rock tank nearly full of sweet water that seeped from beneath a ledge and collected into the natural basin.

Just below the tank, tucked in close against the rock that nature had partially hollowed, were some berry bushes and a low-growing flowery shrub Longarm had never seen before. Hummingbirds with iridescent green and gold throats shrieked and fought around the blossoms, and the berries had already been thoroughly ransacked by other birds.

A much less often used footpath continued past the tank and up into a narrow cut in the rock.

This country was ugly to the passerby, but it held surprises. Longarm drank deeply from the cool, shaded water in the tank before he went back down to the brown.

That experience almost but not quite prepared him for the Kiowa-Apache agency when he finally reached it.

The headquarters was set into a short, broad valley, another jewel dropped into the middle of barren, gray surroundings.

At the head of the valley a thin waterfall tumbled off the heights to the west, to form a creek that someone had dammed to create a sparkling blue lake of three or so acres in extent.

Cedar grew on the slopes of the valley bowl, and a thick stand of pine stood near the head above the creek.

The agency buildings were enough to be considered a small town or village, set above and to the south of the lake.

There was no sign of hide lodges or wickiups or hogans or jacales, but a number of cabins had been built of logs and scattered around the valley. The wagon road ended here, but paths that could be comfortably negotiated by saddle horses led upward from the valley in half a dozen different directions. A few led down as well toward the distant plains, which were easily visible for countless miles to the east. The elevation here gave a view all the way to the Pecos and to the Llano beyond it.

It was a hell of a fine location. Well worth hanging onto.

Longarm stopped there for a moment, thoroughly enjoying the views in any direction he chose to look. Then he nudged the brown into motion again.

He was still nearly a mile out on the slowly descending road when a bunch of children playing in front of a long, low building saw him and set up a cry. What with the shape of the valley and the clarity of the air here he could easily hear their voices although he could not make out the words. The children ran inside the building. A moment later a woman emerged and ran across the compound to another log building. That building would have to be the headquarters itself, Longarm judged from the Stars and Stripes hanging limp on a pine flagpole in front of it.

Longarm bumped the horse into a rocking chair lope and covered the rest of the distance quickly. He was greeted in front of the headquarters by a thin, bespectacled man and two young women. The only Indians in sight were the flock of children, who had scurried inside the other major building, but who were all now peering out through the door and every available inch of window space. The kids looked solemn, he thought, possibly even frightened.

Just in case the children were scared of him he gave them a friendly wave and took the time to light a cheroot before he stepped down from the horse and introduced himself to the agency staff.

"Thank God," the man said. He came forward and offered his hand. "I am Daniel Farady, Marshal, agent here. This is my wife Linda." He pointed toward a tall, slat-thin woman with brown hair. "And Meg Morrison, our schoolteacher."

Longarm took his hat off to greet the ladies.

"Excuse me if you please, gentlemen. I want to go reassure the children that all is well."

Longarm nodded to Miss Morrison again, and she hurried across the compound toward the waiting kids.

He watched her go. It would have been difficult not to. She was as unexpected here—and as lovely—as the valley setting itself. Meg Morrison was only average in height, and there was no way to judge what her figure might be beneath the severe dress she wore, but she had a kind of presence that went beyond outward appearance, even at first look.

And her outward appearance was nothing to sneeze at.

Her hair was done severely tight, entirely proper and plain, but no plain style could hide the color of it. Longarm was not quite sure if he would call it a dusky blond or a pale brown, or quite what. There were hints and highlights of red in it, and gold, or maybe it was more of a bronze.

And why the hell was he standing there staring after a pretty woman, anyway?

Actually, he knew the answer to that one. He just hoped it was not obvious to Mr. and Mrs. Farady. He tried to put his mind back on business.

"I hope you can give me a better idea of what is going on here than I was able to get in Cottonwood," he told the agent. "All I heard down there was that your Kiowa-

Apache have put a curse on them and they all know it's so because they all saw it done. I know that sounds strange, but . . ." He spread his hands.

Farady sighed and looked at his wife. "That is my fault, I'm afraid, Marshall."

"Longarm," he corrected.

"All right." Farady sighed again. "Why don't you come inside, Longarm? Missus, would you prepare something for the marshal to drink."

Farady took Longarm inside. His wife trailed behind them.

The headquarters building was the largest at the agency, but the office portion that they entered was quite small. Longarm judged that the agent's living quarters must be under the same roof.

Farady seated himself behind a battered desk, and Longarm settled for a decidedly uncomfortable wooden chair in front of it.

"About this curse business, Longarm," Farady said unhappily. "I hope you understand that my intentions were the best, sir. Only the best."

There was likely no point in prompting the fellow to get to it, Longarm decided. Better to let Farady explain in his own way.

"It was in late winter, you understand, which here is at the end of the growing season for most garden crops. My Ka-Ays, that's what I call them for convenience, Ka-Ays . . . my Ka-Ays were preparing for their first real harvest using modern methods, and they were quite proud of themselves, I must say. Very quick learners, these Kay-Ays, and very willing. Anyway, you see, they were wanting to have a celebration. A pagan rite, of course, but I try to allow them their own ways to a certain extent."

Longarm thought Farady sounded virtuous and proud of himself about that.

"It was my idea, since we live in such close proximity

49

to Cottonwood and do our purchasing there, it was my idea that we should invite the ... uh ... local whites to this celebration. To get acquainted, so to speak." He sighed. "It truly was my intent that the white and red communities become ... well ... neighbors. With all that implies."

Longarm looked around for someplace to deposit the ashes from his cheroot, but there was nothing suitable in view and Farady did not notice. He had to settle for tapping them into his palm.

"A good many of the people from Cottonwood did attend," Farady went on, unaware. "Quite a few, really. My young Ka-Ays had spent more than a week hunting so we could feed them all. Had quite a spread too, I must say. Antelope, rabbit, deer. Some ... uh ... stew ingredients I did not question. Quite sumptuous, really."

Longarm was beginning to think that Farady would welcome any excuse to delay coming to the point of this tale.

"The Ka-Ays were quite excited by it all. They thought this was their introduction into polite society, one might say. A welcome into the white world, you see."

Longarm nodded and waited patiently.

"They were ..."

Farady was granted another delay when his wife appeared with a tray and pitcher. She poured a thin fruit drink of some sort for them. Longarm tasted the stuff. He would have much preferred something stronger. Water would have done. He sipped at the stuff without comment.

"Where was I?" Farady asked after his wife left without thanks except from Longarm. "Oh, yes. The ceremony. The Ka-Ays were on their very best behavior. They prepared an enormous fire and painted themselves all over. Not war paint, you understand. Strictly ceremonial, although I suppose the people of Cottonwood would not have understood the difference. Now I realize I should have forbidden the paint, but it is much too late for that.

"It was really quite a gala occasion, Longarm. Quite gala. The Ka-Ays danced and chanted, and the white guests ate. I thought everything was going quite well. Then a group of young Ka-Ays from the Snake Society put on a dance that involved a great deal of loud chanting and foot-stamping and the use of a certain number of . . . well, of live rattlesnakes. They had captured the snakes without my knowledge or consent, I assure you.

"And one of the boys in the Snake Society, quite illegally of course, had been drinking tizwin or eating cactus buds or something. I never have gotten a straight answer on that. Suffice it to say that the lad was not being himself. He was handling one of the snakes and gestured toward a white girl with the creature." Farady shuddered himself at the thought of either the snake or the girl or the young Indian . . . or something.

"The girl became frightened and screamed, and her father struck the Ka-Ay boy. Most unfortunate. I am assured that the lad was only being playful, but neither the girl nor her father knew that at the time. Well, by then the damage was done. All the Ka-Ays became sulky because the white man had hit one of their tribe, and the whites became upset because they thought the boy was threatening the girl with the snake. There were angry words spoken on both sides, and I am afraid that one of the old Ka-Ays who still does not accept white ways said something in their pagan tongue and pointed a staff at the girl's father in what I must say was a most threatening manner, and then all the Ka-Ays became even more sulky and left their own party. And the white guests became frightened, and someone kicked over a basket and let a lot of snakes out onto the ground. Which the white men quickly dispatched with their revolvers, of course, because there were a lot of children around. Only white children by then, although there had been Ka-Ay children playing with them until the fuss started.

"And then a few weeks later someone in Cottonwood

came down sick and died and then another, and there was a rumor that these people had died of a poison like a rattlesnake venom and that it was the result of that old fool of a Ka-Ay putting a curse on all the whites because that one man had struck the Ka-Ay boy." Farady ran his palm over his scalp. The man was probably not more than thirty, but already his hair was thinning.

"That is nonsense about the curse, of course. The old fellow told me so."

"Can't you get him to explain that to the people in Cottonwood?" Longarm asked. "If he and the boy would just explain . . ."

"I thought of that, of course, but the old man—his name is Nathan; they have all adopted white names since they moved here—but old Nathan got his back up when I tried to question him, and now he refuses to speak to any white man. As for the boy, he ran off shortly after the incident. I've no idea where he went or why. He simply disappeared one day when he was supposed to be on herding duty."

"What about the tribal leaders? Couldn't they explain it to the people in Cottonwood?"

"I suggested that, but that was some time after the rumors had started. The falsehoods had had time to take root, I suppose, and no one wanted to listen. I tried several times. Then a Texas Ranger showed up. I assume the people called him in to protect them from my Ka-Ays. Just as I asked for your assistance. Since then, though, I haven't been able to get anyone in Cottonwood to listen to a word I say to them about my Ka-Ays. Not one word, sir."

"I can sure believe that," Longarm said. "They aren't feeling real friendly right now."

"Frankly, Marshal, I am concerned. There have been rumors in town about . . . well, about punitive action against my Ka-Ays. Fortunately the Ka-Ays do not know about those rumors, or I fear they might very well revert to

52

their former savage ways. I am told they can be quite difficult if they choose."

"So I've heard," Longarm said drily. Difficult. That was one way to put it. Longarm was sure Farady was worried about the safety and well-being of his Indians. Except that Longarm and Ned Sharply would probably be in agreement about one thing. If a shooting scrap broke out, there would damn sure have to be concern spread around for the people down in Cottonwood too.

And Longarm hadn't come here to choose up sides and protect just those people with one skin color. He was interested in keeping both sides healthy.

Longarm stubbed his cheroot out against his boot sole and tucked the butt into his palm for safekeeping until he figured out what to do with the damn thing. "For a man who hasn't any contact with the town lately, you seem to stay up on the rumors in Cottonwood."

"There is no trick to that," Farady explained. "Miss Morrison's brother is the schoolmaster in Cottonwood. When she accepted the agency posting, James helped her move out here. The people of Cottonwood learned that he was a qualified teacher also and asked him to stay. So we do have one source of information, although I believe James is not in the full confidence of the townspeople because of his connections here. On the other hand, children do speak quite freely about their elders."

"That could be handy," Longarm said.

Farady shrugged. "I hadn't thought about it, actually."

Longarm stood. "I'd like to set up here for a while if you have room for me. I might be wanting to come and go, but I'll want a base of operations someplace. If that's convenient for you."

"Of course, Marshall. Anything we can do. The entire agency is at your disposal."

That certainly was a different attitude from the one he had found down in Cottonwood.

Farady clapped his hands sharply, and an Indian woman came out from the living quarters end of the place. She was the first grown Kiowa-Apache Longarm had seen on the reservation. She was wearing an apron.

"You want the Missus Farady, sir?"

"No, Anita, I want you to show Marshal Long to the visitors' house."

Anita nodded and stood patiently watching Longarm.

Longarm thanked Farady and touched the brim of his hat toward Anita. "If you'll just show me where it is, ma'am, I'll lead the horse over there."

"Oh, no. I take. Come this way, please, sir."

Longarm followed her out into the glare of the sun.

Chapter 6

Longarm was waiting outside the schoolhouse when the day's school session ended. The children came running out, wide-eyed and exuberant in their release from confinement. He could not help thinking how similar the scene would be down in Cottonwood where another Morrison was the teacher. Puppies, indeed.

After the stampede of small bodies had slackened, he checked carefully to make sure he would not get trampled by the tail end of it, then went inside the school building. Meg Morrison was at the chalkboard wiping it clean with a damp cloth. She did not see him, so he had a moment to stand and admire her. She was an admirable-looking woman. He would have guessed her age at somewhere in the mid-twenties, which was unusually old for a woman to remain single in country like this. Still, some women, teachers in particular, he had noticed, seemed to enjoy a single life, and perhaps this Meg was among them.

She finished cleaning the chalkboard, picked up a book and a fresh stick of chalk, and began writing the next day's lessons in a bold, clear hand.

Longarm took a step forward, deliberately letting his boot heel strike hard against the puncheon floor. Miss Morrison turned.

She smiled when she saw him. "Marshal Long. You should have come a few minutes earlier. The children are quite desperately curious about Long Arm. That was what they called you for some reason, Long Arm."

He explained his nickname to her. "Can't figure how they would know about it, though," he said. "Far as I can recall, I've never met a Kiowa-Apache before."

"Children hear more than most grownups think they do, Marshal. And there seems to be an exceptionally active exchange of information among all the reservations. Sometimes the children tell me the most amazing things about happenings at the reservations in the Indian Territories, even all the way up into the Dakotas. I used to be skeptical of their wild stories. Until I realized that some of the things they were telling me about . . . if garbled versions, at times . . . were the same things I would read about in the newspapers weeks or months later. So I am no longer quite the skeptic I used to be. Would you have a seat, marshal? I won't be but a few minutes here. Then we can talk."

"Thank you. But you might as well call me Longarm too, Miss Morrison."

"If you would prefer, Longarm." Her voice was pleasant but neutral. He noticed that she did not suggest he call her Meg.

Miss Morrison turned back to her chalkboard, and Longarm took a seat at the largest desk he could find in the classroom. At that, his knees were jammed against the underside of the writing surface, and he felt like he was one of those little toy sailing ships crammed into a small bottle.

The next day's lessons were heavily weighted toward

instruction in English, with a very few arithmetic problems thrown in.

The classroom was very much like any other he had ever seen, down to the portrait of Washington tacked high on the wall. Beside the standard Washington lithograph was a smaller photographic portrait of Daniel Farady, and flanking Washington on the other side a framed sketch of an Indian.

"Who's the gentleman with the feathers?" Longarm asked when Miss Morrison was done.

"His name is Wash-to-Nah-Tah. Or something like that. I am really quite awful with the Kay-Ay language," Miss Morrison said. "I think he was the last great war chief of the Ka-Ays, but I could be wrong about that too. Only the very littlest of the children will talk about him at all, and I don't believe they are very clear about it themselves. My older children either say nothing at all when I ask them or they tell me the most outrageous fibs. Not that they are liars. I've never found a more honest group of children anywhere. They tell me these impossible things in such a way that I know they are making up the stories from whole cloth. I believe that is their way of very politely refusing to say anything but letting me know that they mean no offense."

Longarm shrugged. "I guess both sides got things to get used to. How long've you been here, Miss Morrison?"

"Since last autumn. Although it feels like only yesterday. There is so much to do and so few hours in the day. I do enjoy it, though. The children are marvelous, such quick learners and so diligent in their studies. Really quite rewarding to work with. And the country is ever so much more lovely than I expected to find here."

"You sound like you are happy here."

"As I should, Marshal. I am."

He smiled at her.

"Was there something I could help you with, Marshal?

57

Not that I am not enjoying talking with you. But I shouldn't want to delay your mission if there was something I could help with."

"Oh, Mr. Farady was telling me about your brother. I was hoping you could introduce me to him soon. Mr. Farady told me how this curse thing got started, but I need to find out what is really happening. Those people in Cottonwood did die from something, you know. Come to think of it, I forgot to ask Farady, but have any of the . . . uh . . . Ka-Ays died? Like from a disease? If there is some kind of epidemic, why, that could be mistaken for a curse, I guess."

"Let me sort that out. Yes, I would be pleased to introduce you to James. I believe you shall find him more enlightened and receptive to your inquiries than most of the people in Cottonwood. No, there is certainly no curse. But no epidemic either. No Ka-Ays have died since I arrived, and I believe they have lost no one since they moved onto the reservation. I wish I could be of more help to you, Marshal."

"Longarm," he said.

"Oh, yes. Sorry." Her smile was still pleasant, still neutral.

"There is one more thing you could help with," he said.
"Yes?"

"I'm just curious, really, but I've been here half the afternoon and the only Kiowa-Apache I've seen are your school children and the lady who works at the Farady house. Where are all the Ka-Ays?"

"Working, of course. They are really quite intent on adopting civilized ways, Longarm. Including a good Presbyterian work ethic. Most of the women will be working in the fields below the valley. They have performed absolute marvels to irrigate the benchland down there. The water flows out of this valley and used to be soon lost underground or to evaporation, but they have channeled and

58

controlled it for irrigation purposes. There are crops that can be raised the year around in this climate, the cooler-weather crops like peas and beans during the winter, those are practically staples, and the hot-weather crops like squash and melons in the fields now.

"And the men would be up in the hills tending the livestock or hunting. The government provided the tribe with seed herds of cattle, sheep, and goats, and of course they have been raising horses for generations. They've brought in some stallions on loan from the government Remount Service to upgrade the horse herds using the Ka-Ay mares."

Longarm noticed that, unlike many single women, young women in particular, Miss Morrison found no discomfort in speaking about stallions and mares. From time to time he had heard some of the damnedest, mind-twisting circumlocutions out of single women who were trying to make a point without using any word that could be directly construed to tell the sex of a farm animal. He liked Meg Morrison's matter-of-fact speech much better.

"Do they all live in this valley?"

"By no means," she said. "There are Ka-Ays scattered through the mountains all through the reservation. There are any number of hospitable spots like this where people can live, and some that are not so hospitable, for that matter. I have a good many of the children here, but not all by any means. Although we hope to improve on that in the future."

"They stick pretty much to the mountains?"

"That surprised me too as I am told they came here from plains country to the east. But then, it was not so many generations ago that their forebears came from country very much like this. So I suppose it should not have been so surprising. The Ka-Ays are very long on tribal traditions, you know."

"Most Indian nations are," he said.

"I have no opinion about that. The Ka-Ays are my first experience with Indians."

"I expect I'd better go," Longarm said. He eased carefully out of the school desk. "I promised the Faradys to take supper with them, and I must say I don't want to be late. Been eating too much of my own cooking lately. When would you expect to see your brother again?"

"I hadn't expected to see him until Saturday. I generally drive down Saturday mornings and spend most of Sunday in town. We used to go to services Sunday mornings, but of course that was before poor Reverend Thomas died."

"The preacher died?"

"Oh my, yes. He was one of those supposed to have been killed by the Ka-Ay curse."

"No one mentioned that. Just the woman and kids."

"And Reverend Thomas."

"A woman, some kids, and the preacher. No wonder folks are riled."

"I understand that. We all do. We sympathize. But, Marshal, the Ka-Ays are *not* responsible."

"No, ma'am. But then I'm not the one who needs to be convinced of that. One more embarrassing question, if you don't mind."

"Yes?"

"You said you'd normally be going down Saturday. Miss Morrison, I have completely forgot what day of the week this would be."

She laughed. It was the first laughter he had heard from her, and he liked the sound of it. "This is Thursday, Marshal."

He opened his mouth to speak, but she got there first.

"I know. Longarm. I will try to remember that."

"Okay."

"Would you want me to go to town sooner than Saturday?"

"No, ma'am. Day after tomorrow will be soon enough. I'll have some things to do up here until then."

"Very well then, Longarm." She stepped forward and offered her hand for him to shake. "If you are busy or prefer not to drive down with me, you can meet me at James's house any time from Saturday noon until midafternoon Sunday. He lives in one of the few 'dobes in Cottonwood. The little house on the west edge of town."

"I'll find it," he said.

"But I am sure I shall see you again before then, Longarm."

"I hope so, Miss Morrison."

He headed back to the log house he had been given for the duration of his visit. He barely had time enough to get cleaned up and into a fresh shirt—if he had a fresh shirt left, come to think of it; he had left home shy in that department—before he would be expected at the Faradys' for dinner.

Apparently Farady and his wife were teetotalers. An after-dinner drink in their home was tea, laced if the guest wished with sugar and/or canned milk. No lemon. Tea was fine, Longarm figured, if you were sick. He wasn't sick.

By the time he walked back to the guest house he was damn sure ready for a drink to warm his belly for the night ahead, but he had nothing in his bag and it was beginning to look like there were no substitutes available on the reservation.

That was a federal law, of course, the sale of alcoholic beverages to or use of them by Indians being prohibited by act of Congress.

But, dang it, there were laws and then there were laws. Some of them a fellow just naturally resisted.

It was dark by the time all the politenesses were over with and Longarm could look forward to some privacy. It was not that the Faradys were inhospitable or anything like that. It was just that Mrs. Farady hardly ever said anything, and Daniel was boring. Longarm could live with that. He did, though, feel some pleasure now at the prospect of his own company for the rest of the evening.

There was a lamp burning inside the guest house when he approached it. Probably Anita or one of the other Ka-Ay servants had been sent over to prepare the place for him. He had discovered during the course of the evening that the Faradys were very well attended by Kiowa-Apache serving women.

He was yawning as he pulled the front door open.

The yawn stopped in mid-stretch as the door swung wide, and Longarm's hand leaped for the butt of the Colt.

Someone was in there waiting for him.

"Ho, Long Arm." Or the man might have said "whoa"; he was not sure which. Either way...

Longarm held his fire and peered inside the place.

The crowd sorted itself out to half a dozen adult male Kiowa-Apache. The one who had spoken was standing. The rest were seated patiently on the sides of Longarm's bed. His first thought was not kind, but he couldn't help it: He hoped none of them had lice.

The bunch certainly looked friendly enough. He shoved the double-action Colt back into his holster and stepped inside.

"Good evening."

The man who seemed to be the leader of this delegation stepped forward and solemnly offered his hand. "You are Long Arm," he said in a deep, slow voice.

"I am," Longarm agreed.

"I am George O'Hara."

Just where George might have come up with a name like that one mystified Longarm, but if it was all right with George it was certainly all right with Custis.

George O'Hara would have been considered tall for an Apache but about average for a Kiowa at five-ten or a bit more. His skin tone was several shades darker than the northern plains Indians Longarm was more familiar with, and his face was deeply wrinkled. He might have been anywhere from his early forties to his late fifties—or ten years in either direction from that range, too, for all Longarm knew. It was hard to judge.

He wore clothing that would have been normal on any cowhand with two minor exceptions at the north and south extremities. On his feet he had tall, Apache-style moccasin boots. And his hair was left long and braided on both sides, with bits of carved seashell and puffs of fur and pieces of silver-mounted turquoise worked into the braids.

It was his eyes, though, that told the tale about George O'Hara. They were large and intelligent. They were also searching deep into Longarm's.

The two men shook hands, and Longarm looked straight into George's inspection, giving the man all the time he wanted to make up his mind.

After a moment, George grunted with satisfaction and broke the handshake. He took a step back and turned to say something to the other five men in a guttural tongue that meant nothing to Longarm. When he turned back to Longarm he said, "I am president of the Ka-Ay tribal council." There was no hint of smile on him when he said that, but Longarm thought he could see a flicker of amusement in O'Hara's eyes, way down deep. Longarm guessed that the title was one Daniel Farady had decided on for his Ka-Ays. Whatever, O'Hara did not seem to mind either it or the conversational shorthand "Ka-Ay" that Farady had also invented. But then, the designation Kiowa-Apache was a white man's invention, too. The only real difference was that it had been thought up by a different white man.

Longarm introduced himself.

"It is good," O'Hara said. "We asked for you to come. You are known as a white who does not lie and does not hate. You are a man of respect."

"Thank you."

"You will help us kill the Texans when they come," O'Hara said.

"No, I will not. I didn't come here to kill. I came here to help."

One of the Indians on the bed said something, and that caused a round of emotional chatter. O'Hara seemed to be the youngest of the crowd, but when he spoke, after letting the others talk for a few minutes, the rest of them shut up. They looked like they didn't like it, but they did shut up. O'Hara offered no explanations or translations of whatever they had been discussing.

"If we must kill the Texans, you will not interfere," O'Hara said.

"Nope, wrong again. I'll interfere all I can if it comes to that. To keep them from attacking you or to keep you from jumping them." Longarm checked his pockets. He didn't have enough cheroots for everybody, so he got a fistful out of his carpetbag and offered them all around. All the Indians accepted a smoke except for one very old, very stern-looking Ka-Ay who looked vaguely familiar. Longarm wondered if he might have seen that one with the Kiowa or the Comanche at some point in the past. He was sure he had never met him, but he might have seen him.

Of the bunch, the elderly party was the only one dressed completely in the old style, buckskins and fur and gaudy adornments. All the rest were mostly, if not completely, dressed in white man's clothes.

Longarm gave the old man a long, deliberate look, making no attempt to hide it. This one, then, who refused to smoke with him, was the one who had reservations about him. This was the leader of the opposition party on George O'Hara's tribal council.

Still looking at the old fellow, Longarm said, "I am Long Arm." The implication was clear enough.

The old boy thought about it for a while. Then he bent a little. He thumped his chest and said, "Nay-Tan." He did not offer his hand to shake, and Longarm did not push it any further. He nodded and turned back to O'Hara.

"You say you do not come to kill," O'Hara said. "Good. We come here to live, not kill. It is as we were told. Long Arm does not whine."

Longarm smiled. "Whine? Pretty fancy word, George. I don't think you learned your English from Miss Morrison over the past few months."

"No," O'Hara said easily. "Many years ago my people took a white prisoner. A missionary. Teacher. We kept him for many months until we learned what he taught. Then we ate him."

He said it with a straight, serious face. But again Longarm could see that hint of twinkle deep in O'Hara's eyes.

Longarm couldn't help himself. He burst out laughing at the absurdity of a plains Indian making like a damned cannibal.

George grinned at him. The others, except for old Nay-Tan, began to smile too. The ice was broken.

Still chuckling, Longarm motioned toward the bed, which was the only place in the room where a person could sit. "Sit down, George. I'd offer you boys something to drink, but I don't have anything with me."

George considered that for a moment, then nodded. Instead of going to the bed to sit, he went to the door and opened it a few inches. He said something through it. A few minutes later a puffing youngster, a boy probably in his teens and dressed totally Indian, came in with a pair of cavalry-issue saddlebags, handed them to O'Hara, and left.

O'Hara opened the flaps and pulled bottles out of both sides of the bags. He handed one to Longarm.

Scotch whisky, by damn, and a good grade of it at that.

It wasn't rye, but it certainly would do as a substitute.

Longarm pulled the cork and saluted first O'Hara and then the rest of the council with the opened bottle. He took a welcome pull on it and handed the bottle to his right.

The Indians circulated it to the right, each drinking in turn. Before it reached O'Hara, though, they passed it back around to the left, this time no one drinking from it, until it reached George. He drank deeply from the bottle and started it on its right-ward passage once again. They did not happen to be in a lodge at the moment, but they were following the old custom anyway. The Ka-Ays were an interesting blend of new ways and old, Longarm thought.

When the bottle reached him the second time he drank from it.

After that the talk went on well into the night, with even old Nay-Tan participating now and then.

Chapter 7

Longarm woke with a headache. He sure couldn't understand where he might have picked that up. Not on an Indian reservation where there wasn't any whiskey. Fortunately George O'Hara had left behind a bottle of the remedy for what ailed him. He took a nip of it and felt a little better. He dressed and went out to face the morning.

The agency headquarters was as deserted now as it had been the previous afternoon. Apparently the Ka-Ays were every bit as diligent as Miss Morrison had indicated. They were already off at their fields and their herds. Longarm could see some shadowy movements inside the school building, although surely classes would not have started yet. Behind the Faradys place Anita was bent over a washtub. Longarm ambled over to her.

"Good morning, ma'am," he said with a touch of his hatbrim.

She blinked and looked shyly away from him. Apparently she was not used to receiving courtesies from white men.

"I was hoping you could do something for me, Anita."

"I do."

"I was thinking maybe you could do up some laundry for me. I'd pay you, of course."

"I do," she said again. "No pay. I do."

"No pay, no wash. Wouldn't be fair."

She hesitated, then nodded. "I do. You want food now?"

"That'd be real nice, ma'am."

"I bring." She left her washing and trotted toward the back of the Faradys' place. Longarm walked down to the bank of the pond while he was waiting. The water was clear, and he could see the dark, darting shapes of fish in the depths. This was a fine spot. Some government clerk would really be furious if he ever learned what good land he had assigned to the Kiowa-Apache.

Anita brought Longarm a heaping plate of johnnycakes and fried salt pork, and he sat beside the lake while he tucked into it. When he was done Anita took the plate away for him.

Miss Morrison came outside a little while later to ring the school bell. She waved toward Longarm but did not come over. Her pupils were streaming toward the schoolhouse from the nearby cabins, and her work day was beginning.

About time mine started too, Longarm told himself. Sitting beside a pretty lake was pleasant but not productive. He stood, brushed off the seat of his britches, and headed for the corral.

He had not actually been loafing the morning away. While he sat he was trying to come up with some logical reason for those people down in Cottonwood to have died.

Something had killed them. And both the folks in Cot-

68

tonwood and the people here at the reservation agreed that it was not an ordinary disease that killed them.

He had tried to talk about that with George O'Hara and the Kay-Ay council last night, but they had been evasive. Polite, but evasive. Just like Miss Morrison told him their kids did in school when she asked them something they did not want to answer, when Longarm brought up the subject of the deaths, George O'Hara had given him one of those straight-faced, solemn looks and said, "Curse, of course. Ancient curse from early times killed them."

Ancient curse, indeed. Hell's bells, in ancient times neither the Texans nor the Kiowa-Apache had been in this country. A few Mexicans, maybe, and some Mescaleros, but none of these folks of either skin color.

Yet some damn thing had killed those people. There was no denying that, whatever the Ka-Ay council wanted to pretend.

Longarm grunted to himself. He couldn't figure why the Ka-Ays would be reluctant to talk about it, anyway. But then, there were some things about Indian thought processes that were just plain different. That a white man, no matter how well intentioned, just plain couldn't grab hold of.

Or maybe that was too strong a way to put it. Custis Long probably shouldn't count himself a representative of the whole white race. Maybe there was somebody somewhere who could see through the differences. But he could say for certain-sure that he couldn't fathom it. Nobody could dispute him on that.

He frowned and snapped the cinch strap tight under the McClellan. None of this idle speculation was getting the job done.

And part of the problem was that he really did not know where to go to *get* it done, damn it.

First things first, he told himself. One step at a time.

The highest ladder only gets climbed one rung at a time. The toughest knot has to be loosened strand by strand.

He stepped into the saddle, clamped his knees tight while the brown got the morning kinks out of its back, then turned the horse toward Cottonwood.

He'd had a chance already to talk with Ned Sharply and Daniel Farady and George O'Hara. And if there weren't going to be any easy answers, well, he would just have to go look for the hard ones.

Longarm followed his nose, taking one of the paths to the south of the waterfall and climbing out of the valley onto the higher ground above.

The thin stream of water that fed the fall and the lake below it came out of the ground, appearing in full force from under a maze of jagged boulders that lay at the foot of a cliff. It ran through a small cirque above the valley, the floor of this smaller bowl grassy and filled now with a flock—flock? herd, he thought—of hairy goats. Several teenage boys were in charge of the goats, although they seemed to be spending their time practicing with bows and arrows more than in watching the goat herd. Or flock. They waved when they saw Longarm.

He rode south, following the rise and fall of the rims above the foothills. The terrain here was rugged and gray, sparsely watered. Yet there was grass appearing in patches wherever there was moisture or shade or whatever whim of nature it was that said aye or nay to the growth. Scarce as the dry bunchgrasses were, there was enough of it that livestock could thrive in this high country, given enough land to graze.

Longarm passed several Ka-Ay herds as he went, the goats close to the headquarters valley, small herds of cattle and sheep farther away.

He saw only one Ka-Ay dwelling, a daub and wattle affair that was closer to being a jacale than anything else he could recognize, but he might have passed dozens more without noticing them in the jagged, rocky country.

Old paths wound through and among the rocks. Paths carved possibly for centuries by wild game, probably by wild Indians and now by reservation Ka-Ay and domesticated livestock.

The rocks themselves were wind- and water-carved, taking on eerie shapes, shot through with niches and blowholes and dark openings that might have been mere pockets in the limestone or might as easily have been caves that ran deep into the rock. He did not try to investigate them.

Finding a path south was no problem. The only difficulty was in deciding which path to follow.

He had come up from Cottonwood on the road. He had been curious if there were other routes. Others? There were hundreds. If Sharply and his Texans wanted to make a raid on the reservation, Longarm hoped he would not have to intercept them up here. An army could travel over these mountains, and each individual foot soldier could have his own separate path to follow if he damn well wanted one.

Longarm held to the east side of the rims and had no trouble spotting the dry watercourse below that he could follow on down to Cottonwood. There, too, he had almost unlimited choices in what route he wanted to take down to the flat country. The Guadalupes were rugged, but they were by no means a fortress. They could be invaded at almost any point a man chose. Damned unfortunate, the way Longarm saw it, particularly if he was right about Ned Sharply's intentions.

He picked a descending path virtually at random and turned the horse down it.

Near the bottom it was easy to see how the dry creekbed had come to be there. The path he was following angled alongside a wide, vee-bottomed chute that had been carved by fast-running water. During wet years, during the melt after a snowy winter or after a heavy rain, the chute would be a regular millrace, and the creek would likely turn into a real if short-lived river.

Even at this time of year there was another natural tank at the bottom of the chute with tepid water still standing in it and a small outflow trickling down over the rocks until it reached the sand below and sank underground.

The tank was too awkwardly placed for a horse to reach it, although droppings nearby showed that it was visited by coyotes and sheep, very likely wild desert bighorns down here, as Longarm had not seen any sign of Ka-Ay stock for more than an hour. He was not even sure that the reservation land ran this far south. Probably he had left the federal lands several miles back.

He stopped at the bottom and watered the brown from his canteens and collapsible bucket, then climbed back up to the tank on foot rather than drink the stale water from the remaining canteen.

Habitual caution made him pause to look and listen to the country around him before he bent to drink from the still water in the tinaja.

He drank, then made a face and wiped at his lips with the back of his hand, regretting that he hadn't settled for the water in his canteen.

The water in the tank must have been standing too long, or possibly something had knocked some weeds or rocks down into it. He looked, but the bottom seemed to be clear enough except for some sand and pea gravel.

Whatever, the water tasted like shit. Like garlic, to be more accurate about it. Like a sweetish, off-flavored garlic. Certainly it did not taste good.

He worked his jaw back and forth until he got some saliva to flow, swished it around inside his mouth, and spat. That helped a little. Frowning, he climbed back down to the level ground where the horse was cropping at some dry, sun-cured grass.

"Count yourself lucky," he told the creature. It flicked an ear toward him but continued eating.

He took the last canteen down, rinsed his mouth, and spat out the first swig, then drank until he was satisfied.

The horse protested just a little when he remounted. Eating was much more enjoyable than working. But it did not offer to buck and likely would not again until tomorrow's first saddling. Longarm squeezed the brown into a walk. Then, as they cleared the last of the rocks dumped down out of the chute, he bumped the animal into a slow lope through the level sand of the creekbed.

He had things to do and places to go that did not involve playing in a rockpile.

Chapter 8

Longarm reached the outskirts—such as they were—of Cottonwood early in the afternoon. From down in the creekbed, which in many places was a dozen feet lower than the level of the surrounding ground, the only way he knew he was passing the outlying ranch buildings and hardscrabble subsistence farms was by their wells. The buildings themselves might be set well back from the creek where he could not see them from the bottom of the wash, and there might or might not be a path carved down to the sand, but invariably there would be a rock casing set some-where near the top of the bank to mark some homesteader's dug well. The wells were prudently placed out of the creekbed itself but were always situated as near it as possi-ble.

Apparently the underground flow of water was only de-pendable near the sometime surface flow course.

Eventually he reached the pond in the bend of the bed

and knew he was at Cottonwood. He had completely passed by much of the town without ever once being able to see so much as a rooftop from the level where he was riding.

He reined the brown left and angled it up onto hard ground again.

It was past lunchtime and he was hungry. He could have made it down much quicker by the road but did not consider the time to have been wasted. He did not want to have a repeat of the discomforts of the cafe. He settled instead for stopping in at the mercantile and buying a hunk of rat cheese and some hard crackers, then headed for a saloon to get a beer to wash his dry lunch down.

In both the store and the saloon he received service. Strictly business, with no hint of cordiality, but service nonetheless. It was something.

"You wouldn't have any rye on hand, would you?" he asked when he was done eating and was ready for something more substantial than a beer to settle the meal. Normally he would have specified his preference for Maryland distilled rye, but by now he knew better than to press his luck in Cottonwood.

"No rye," the bartender told him. "I have some decent corn whiskey that my brother sends out from Kentucky. I could draw you a bottle o' that if you want."

Longarm wanted. He had left George O'Hara's Scotch back at the reservation guest house and wanted something to put into his saddlebags.

While the barman was decanting a quart of the corn from a small keg into a once-used bottle, Longarm leaned on the bar and took note of the homemade appearance of the small keg.

The thing was crudely but effectively manufactured. What interested him, though, was that it had no brands or metal stamp indents on it that he could see. Probably the whiskey was as homemade as the keg it came in. Sent by a

75

brother in Kentucky? Likely not tax-paid and therefore illegal under federal law.

Longarm said nothing about that at the moment but tucked the information away in the event of future need. There could come a time when he might want some leverage on a Cottonwood local. The bartender had just given him that if he should want to use it.

For the time being, though, he had no intention of rousting a local to no real purpose. Better to let that one slide.

He accepted the bottle and paid for it, then walked back out into the afternoon sunshine.

The word must have been around already that the nuisance was back in town. When Longarm came out of the saloon Ned Sharply and Junior were idling on the sidewalk across the street. Ned seemed to be extremely busy cleaning his fingernails. Junior was carefully dismantling a mesquite bean pod. Neither of them was paying any attention to the federal deputy fussing at his saddlebags on the far side of the street. Or so it seemed, anyway. Their appearance was quite coincidental. Sure it was. Longarm smiled at them and waved, but they did not see. Not to admit to, anyway.

To hell with 'em, Longarm told himself. He swung onto the brown and rode toward the west end of town.

He stopped at the sagging sale barn again and stripped the saddle off the brown before he turned it loose in the corral.

There was no water for the animal in the trough. Either the thing leaked or it got more use than Longarm had thought.

The last time he had stopped here he had drawn water from the pond down in the creekbed, but that was a hot hike in the afternoon sun. Tipped by the wells he had seen on the way down from the mountain, he looked closer and found what he wanted in a hand-dug well set between the back corner of the old barn and the creek bank. The casing was half hidden by a straggly, struggling lilac bush, or he might have seen it before. There was no beam or pulley over it, but the water level in the well was not more than twenty-five feet below the surface. His catch rope and collapsible bucket reached it easily.

He carried several buckets to the trough for the horse, then drew one more to slosh over his wind-dried face and neck and took a mouthful for himself. He made a sour face and spat the water onto the ground.

Either it was his imagination or the damned stuff had the same flavor—if considerably milder—as that bad water he had run into up at the tank under that rock chute.

Probably just imagination, he told himself. Or an aftertaste left over from that first drink.

He tried the well water again, deliberately this time, swishing the cool fluid from cheek to cheek and paying attention.

No, damn it, he was almost sure he could taste it there. Very faint. Not so unpleasant as that earlier harsh flavor. But there. Garlicky and almost sweet.

Now what kind of weed would do that?

He tried to look down into the bottom of the well, but the water was too deep and the shadows too heavy for him to make anything out for certain. He could not see anything, though. Just as he had found nothing on the bottom of the tank. That he had been certain about.

"Shit," he said again, louder this time.

He tossed the bucket inside the barn and hurried on foot toward town. Ned and Junior had shifted their idling down toward the barn end of town. Now they were loafing on the front porch of a house. Longarm ignored them and walked quickly back toward the store where he had stocked up the other day. That man had at least been semi-friendly.

"Good aft—"

"Do you have a doctor in town?" Longarm interrupted him.

The storekeeper blinked before he answered. "Well, no. Not exactly."

"A druggist, then?"

The storekeeper scratched at a scab beside his nose. "No, not one of them either, exactly."

"What do you have for educated folks in town?" Longarm demanded.

"Well," the man said slowly, pondering as he spoke, "me and Ben Lyle across the street both sell some bottled remedies. You know the kind I mean."

Longarm did, and Dr. Falstaff's Medicated Miracle Tonic was not what he had in mind.

"An' then there's Kyle Johnston. He repairs saddles, harness, like that, an' on the side he does some barbering. Got some regular barber surgeon schooling, Kyle says, so he knows how to set bones an' stop up cuts an' such as that." The man nodded to himself. "Ayuh, I would say that Kyle would be 'bout as close as we got to a doctor. But he'd tell you himself that he wouldn't know how to perscribe medicines. An, if he did, they'd have to be ordered out of El Paso or maybe up from the army doctors down at Fort Davis. Yeah, I'd say one of those would be about the closest real doctors to here."

Damn. Davis or El Paso either one would be days away.

"As for educated folks," the storekeeper went blithely on, completely intent on the answer now that he had gotten started, "I think Charles Johnson—no relation to Kyle, who spells his last name different—I think Charles graduated high school back in Denton and might have spent some time in college too. Then there's . . ."

Longarm was no longer listening. "Do you have a telegraph?" he asked.

The question was a foolish one, but desperate. If he'd thought about it before it was out of his mouth he would have realized that he had seen no telegraph wires since he left Fort Sumner. There would be a line running somewhere to the south, taking message traffic from Fort Davis and from El Paso. But that could be even farther away than Davis.

The storekeeper blinked again. "No. No telegraph. No need for one, when you come right down to it, though there's some folks as have been talking about asking to have a wire run to us. But they're the same folks as want to take up a public subscription an' build a town hall. Though what use we'd have for a town hall, well, nobody else around here seems t' know. But they say—"

Longarm threw a quick thank-you over his shoulder as he left the store, leaving the proprietor rambling slowly to himself.

Longarm needed, positively *needed* someone knowledgeable enough to give him information that was plainly beyond a deputy marshal's capabilities.

It was beginning to look like that could be a hard person to come by in Cottonwood, Texas.

"I hope this won't get you into trouble," Longarm said, "and I apologize for disrupting your schedule. There wasn't any way to hide the visit from anyone, though. I've been watched ever since I got into town."

"Don't worry about that," James Morrison said pleasantly. "I make no attempt to hide my personal beliefs anyway." He laughed. "Besides, I am sure the children were delighted to get the afternoon free. We are near the end of the term, and their attention has not been on their studies in any case."

"Thanks." Once again Longarm found himself squeezed into a seat meant for a pupil half his size.

Morrison pulled a pipe from his pocket and loaded it. "I assume you have something of some importance to discuss with me?"

"Indeed. Excuse me for taking so long to get to the point, but I'm trying to get my own thoughts in order. I don't want to risk raising false fears, maybe causing a panic."

At the use of the word "panic," Morrison's eyebrows went up, but he did not press again. He sat on the front edge of his teacher's desk and took his time about lighting the pipe, giving Longarm time enough to think this through.

Morrison was a handsome man, close enough in age to his sister that Longarm would have found it difficult to decide which of them was the older. The two had the same coloring and the same finely molded features. They even had the same eyes. If he had not already known that they were brother and sister, Longarm suspected he would have been able to guess it.

"Before I go out on this limb," Longarm asked, "do you have any training in chemistry? Or any knowledge of medicine, perhaps?"

James drew on his pipe thoughtfully for a moment. "I took a few courses in rudimentary chemistry in normal school," he said. "Nothing deeper than an imparted ability to challenge youngsters in the sciences, though, I am afraid." He smiled. "And hopefully to stay one short step ahead of the more gifted ones if I apply myself to their questions. As for medicine," he shook his head, "nothing whatsoever. I own a medical home companion encyclopedia that Meaghan and I purchased before we came west, in the event of emergencies, but nothing more than that."

"Damn," Longarm said. "I was hoping . . . well, never mind what I was hoping."

"You sound concerned, Marshal."

"I am," Longarm admitted.

"If it helps, we do have that encyclopedia. It is a rather good one, in two volumes. And I have a few chemistry texts tucked in among the other volumes of my library. When Meaghan and I moved here we sacrificed the bulk of our packing space to books even in preference to clothing. Our theory was that clothing could be obtained anywhere, but the great works of literature are invaluable. We brought as wide a selection as we could manage."

"That might help," Longarm said, also tucking away the knowledge that Meg was a contraction from Meaghan and not from the more ordinary Margaret. He was damn well interested in that lady, although she seemed not to realize it.

James smiled gently. "Don't you agree, though, that I should have some hint of the problem if I am to be of any help?"

"Sorry." Longarm managed a weak smile. "I do seem to be saying that an awful lot, don't I?"

"No problem as far as I am concerned, Marshal, I assure you. I have no pressing appointments this afternoon."

"Okay. You're right. I'll get to the damn point." Longarm took a deep breath. "Mr. Morrison, would you happen to know anything about poisons?"

Chapter 9

"Here . . . no, that couldn't be it. Wait a minute." Morrison was bent over several different books that were spread open on top of his desk. He kept marking his place with a finger and moving to another book, then marking that spot and going back to the first.

Longarm was pacing the floor near the windows with a cheroot clamped between his teeth and a growing impatience in his gut.

"This might be something," Morrison said.

"Yeah?" Longarm crossed the classroom to bend over James Morrison's shoulder.

"This right here."

"Arsenates? What the hell are arsenates?"

Morrison referred to another of the books before he answered. "The arsenate family—lead, sodium, and so forth —is used as a less powerful but much less expensive substitute for arsenic. The arsenate family has commercial and industrial applications such as in taxidermy and hide preservation, as a hardening agent in the molding of lead such as the manufacture of firearms projectiles . . ."

"Firearms projectiles. A fancy way of saying bullets."

"Exactly," Morrison said. "Also, certain modern-day embalming techniques, and so on and so forth."

"So what makes you think this arsenate stuff might be it?"

Morrison gave a nervous glance toward the pitcher of water they had drawn from the well behind the school-house. "According to this one over here, the medical encyclopedia, the arsenates are mildly poisonous. The effects of the poisons, while slow, are cumulative. And they are said to impart a faintly sweet garlic flavor if ingested."

"Well, I'll be a son of a bitch," Longarm said.

"It does sound possible, doesn't it?" Morrison said.

"Sure does. Does your book say anything about natural occurrence of these arsenates? I mean, could this be some kind of mineral deposit that the natural waterflow is tapping?"

Morrison bent over the books again. After a considerable time he sat back in his chair and pinched the bridge of his nose. "I don't believe it could be a natural phenomenon, Longarm. I mean, the books don't say so specifically. But they refer to the processing of the arsenates by chemical means. I guess we could not rule out a natural occurrence, though. I'm sorry. I just can't say for sure."

Longarm pondered the information for a moment. "It was two kids, one woman, and a grown man who've died, right?"

"That is correct," Morrison said.

"Tell me about this preacher."

"Reverend Thomas? He was a lovely man. Meaghan and I attended his services every week."

"That isn't what I meant. Was he a young man?"

"Oh, no. Quite elderly, actually. I've no idea what his

exact age was, but I remember him telling us that he had retired from a pulpit back east, Illinois I believe. Somewhere in Illinois. His daughter is still here. She married a man who has taken land southwest of Cottonwood. Reverend Thomas came here to be close to her after his retirement and accepted the pulpit here when he realized there was no other ordained minister within a hundred miles or so. Why?"

"Think about it," Longarm said.

Morrison looked back down toward his books. After a moment comprehension dawned. "Of course. The arsenates are a slow-acting, cumulative poison of low grade and, if in drinking water, presumably of a low concentration as well. They would act first on the very small or the very weak or the infirm."

"Uh-huh. Makes sense to me."

"The young lady who died lived on a ranch several miles west of here, Longarm. You probably passed it on your way in."

"Closer to the source, then, if somebody's been putting poisonous arsenates into the water. Like up at the tank where I stopped earlier. You'd have to figure that the concentration would be heavier closer to the source of the contamination."

"I agree."

"Jesus," Longarm said. "The shit is really gonna fly when we have to tell folks to quit drinking their well water."

Morrison looked worried. "I don't think you should do that, Marshal."

"Man, I can't find out something like this an' just let people go on poisoning themselves. I have to tell them."

"You have to tell them something, of course. But must it be the whole truth?"

"What're you driving at, James?"

"I know the people of this community, Longarm. Far better than you, of course, but also considerably better than most of them realize. I hear more than they would think, through their children, but please don't pass that around."

It was much the same thing Meg Morrison had told him about the Ka-Ay children's tendency to talk more than the grown folks might want.

"And I am aware of how very close this community is to taking direct and, I might add, violent action. Directed toward Meaghan's Ka-Ays, Longarm."

"I kinda figured as much."

"Believe it. Ranger Sharply wants only an excuse to get into action again against hostile Indians. The only reason he has not been able to prevail so far is that a fair number of people in Cottonwood, particularly the community leaders, are reluctant to be stampeded into believing ghost stories. The idea that some old Indian put a curse on them is a bit hard for the thinking members of the community to accept. And so far they have been able to exert enough influence for restraint that the others, the ones who would follow Sharply, have been held in check."

"I think I hear a ghost in that story. Like maybe the ghost of an unspoken 'but'?"

Morrison smiled. "And so you do, Longarm. Think about it for a moment. If you, we . . . I shouldn't want to absolve myself of the ethical responsibilities here . . . if we should walk out onto the streets of Cottonwood and announce that the water supply has been poisoned, what would the most likely reaction be? The assumption must inevitably be that some human agency has poisoned the water. And who would be the logical suspects? The despised Indians. It would be only natural. Do you honestly believe Ranger Sharply could be held back once people stopped thinking in terms of curses and started looking for objects of vengeance?"

Longarm puffed out his cheeks and exhaled slowly. "Not no way, not no how. They'd be off on their damn raid tonight."

"Exactly," Morrison said.

"But we can't let 'em keep on drinking poisoned water."

"Remember, Longarm, we don't know, I mean we do not absolutely know for certain, that the water is poisoned. We have only supposition and these laymen's volumes to go on. I could very well be wrong about the presence of arsenates in the water. I have neither the means nor the knowledge to test for the substance."

"Are you willing to let more people die while we send samples off to have them analyzed someplace? Hell, man, that could take months. And weeks more to get the information here once they had it." Longarm shook his head. "Maybe I don't have actual proof, James, but I'm not willing to let decent folks die. Not even take the chance of it. I couldn't do that."

It was Morrison's turn to do some thinking. After a moment his shoulders sagged. "You are right, of course. Sorry, but I guess I was willing to make that suggestion as long as the moral responsibility would be yours and not mine. We cannot do it."

"So we got no choice about it. We got to tell them."

"And create panic?"

"If that's what it takes. If I have to I guess I can declare martial law in Cottonwood." He smiled grimly. "Of course I'm the only son of a bitch this side of Fort Davis that'd be handy for the enforcement of that order. But maybe I could get the Ka-Ays to hide out for a while or . . . I don't know . . . some damn thing."

Morrison shook his head. "That wouldn't work either. You haven't spent enough time at the agency to learn very much about the mood there, but believe me, there is a faction there that would like an excuse for a fight too.

George O'Hara is a good man, a foresighted man who is looking to the future for his people. But his is not the only influence on that reservation just as, thank God, Ned Sharply's is not the only influence in town. There are also people like old Nathan. Nay-Tan would rather paint his face one last time and take the fast route to the Happy Hunting Grounds, or whatever the Ka-Ay version of Heaven is supposed to be. If the Ka-Ays were asked to hide, old Nay-Tan and his young wildcats would grab their weapons and their war paint and beg the Texans to come after them."

"Nay-Tan is Nathan? The same one who was supposed to have caused all this trouble to begin with?"

"That's right. Nay-Tan is the Ka-Ay pronunciation of Nathan. Whatever the old bastard's name used to be, he calls himself that now. Virtually all of the Kay-Ays took civilized names before they came here, but I suspect Nay-Tan's has meaning in their own tongue too. Otherwise I am sure he would object to using it. He isn't like George, believe me."

"Of course, all of that's neither here nor there," Long-arm said. "The point right now is getting the people in town to quit poisoning themselves."

"Give me a minute. Surely we can afford that much delay."

"All right."

Longarm walked to the windows and examined the scenery. Not that there was so very much to see. Ned and Junior were across the way, sitting in rocking chairs on the shaded front porch of a house where Longarm had tried to find boarding. If they were actually staying there it was only a coincidence, he was sure. They acted like they weren't paying the least lick of attention to the school, but he knew damn good and well they were aware he was in there. Junior was whittling on a piece of wood, and Ned was sitting with his hat tilted over his eyes and his chin down on his chest. Longarm didn't believe for a minute that the man was napping.

Behind Longarm James Morrison had swiveled his chair around to face the blank chalkboard and was staring toward it. After a while Morrison straightened and turned his chair back toward the desk. "I have an idea," he said.

"If it's even halfway sensible and could save some lives around here, I'll likely grab at it. Spit it out, man."

"What if I put the word around that I've been doing some studying in my medical encyclopedia . . . why, perhaps we might even be able to find some logical culprit to blame the scare on . . . and I tell people I have come to believe that the illnesses are caused by a water-borne disease. Nothing common, of course. Something with a two-dollar name. Something that would mean everyone should stop drinking the well water until we are sure. Surely we could organize water hauls down to the Pecos for our drinking water. It could be a town effort. Get everyone to contribute barrels and teams and wagons. Rotate the duties."

Longarm grinned. "It'd be giving folks something active that they could be doing about the problem. Without them ever knowing what the real problem is."

Morrison looked relieved. So, for that matter, did Longarm.

"I am sure I could pull it off," Morrison said. "The people here are genuinely good people, Longarm. They are concerned parents, very protective of their children. I know if I emphasize that the children are the most at risk, they would go along with it."

"It'd buy me some time, James."

"Time?"

"James, some son of a bitch has put those arsenates in the water. Assuming that's what is doing it, of course. This isn't some ghost or curse we're talking about but a living, breathing, human person. And that kind I can go out and lay hands on."

"Do your part then, Longarm. I'll buy you the time for it."

"Deal," Longarm said with a grin.

The two men shook on it.

It was fairly late in the afternoon before Longarm slipped away from the schoolhouse. Too late for a normal start on the trail, but this was not a normal trip. Longarm did not know how long James Morrison's line of bullshit would hold the folks in Cottonwood and keep them from drinking the water without jumping the Kiowa-Apache about it. He had no time to waste in finding whoever it was who had poisoned the town's water supply.

On the other hand, he was not inclined to be foolish about it. He certainly did not want Ned and Junior Sharply coming along for the ride and perhaps interfering. The less they or anyone else in Cottonwood knew about what was going on, the better for everybody.

He went to the window of the school and stood well back in the shadows while he checked out front.

Ned was still taking his make-believe nap. Or possibly a real one, since he had Junior there to keep watch for him. Sharply could get away with that if he wished. It was a luxury denied to Deputy Long.

Junior continued to whittle on a stick. Either the kid was an almighty slow and deliberate whittler or he had gone through several sticks by now. Finding that information in Morrison's books had taken some time.

Longarm sent a small smile in the direction of the two Sharplys. He wished them a quiet, lazy afternoon.

Then he went to a window in the back wall and slid through it. There was no back door. Poor Junior was likely to get a hell of a chewing out, though, when the two realized Longarm had gotten away from them.

"Remember," Longarm whispered back through the window to Morrison . . . although there probably was no point in whispering; it just seemed the natural thing to do under the circumstances, "when they ask, James, you tell 'em I stopped by an' asked you to get a message up to your sister about . . . oh, hell, I don't know. . ."

"I'll think of something," Morrison assured him.

"Okay. Anyway, I left that message for your sister, then I snuck out this window here. But be sure an' tell them I was only here for a few minutes. They haven't been watching the back, so's they won't know the difference, and that will take some of the suspicion off you when you spin your story for the town. Okay?"

Morrison nodded. "I can handle it. Don't worry. Good luck to you, Longarm."

"To you, too, James. To you and all the folks here, good luck."

Morrison looked grim at the thought of what could happen if he failed.

Without the time he could buy, without Longarm's quick success, Cottonwood, Texas and the entire Kiowa-Apache reservation could explode into warfare.

Both men realized that all too well.

Morrison raised a hand in farwell salute, but by then Longarm was gone.

The brown jogged slowly but steadily through the dry sand of the creekbed. Longarm held his gait to a long jog despite the sense of urgency that was pressing at him. The sand was deep and difficult to move through, and the way might appear to be level but inevitably had to be climbing. It is a simple rule of nature that water must necessarily run downhill, and when you are moving upstream in the flattest-seeming watercourse you must just as naturally be climbing. Longarm had no intention of wearing out the brown at this stage of the game.

He held to the bottom of the sandy bed even though he could have made better time on the harder ground above. Now the steep banks and the fact that the ranches and small outfits to the west of town were set well back from the banks was an asset. He wanted no one to see his passage and mention it to the Sharplys. Much better if he could drop completely out of sight.

He passed the wells set high on the bank and was acutely conscious that he had not yet refilled his canteens. That was something he would have to do at the earliest opportunity.

But *not* at the tainted tank at the base of the rock chute.

The concentration of arsenates had been high in the tank. He had to assume that that was where they were being placed into the water. The same water that flowed underground and eventually reached the drinking wells of Cottonwood.

To check that, though, he simply had to climb upstream, above the tank to the high ground at the head of the chute, and taste the water there. That should prove his point one way or the other.

He passed the last of the outlying ranches and felt more comfortable but continued to ride in the depression of the creekbed. It was coming evening now, and hands from those places would be riding homeward. He did not want any of them to see him either.

The brown reached the gray wall of mountain rock just before dark. Longarm made his camp there, prudently out of the wash, though. The skies were clear, but an unexpected storm during the night, even a rainfall too far away to be seen or heard, could send a torrent down the chute.

He unsaddled and hobbled the brown to turn it loose to graze on the sparse, dry grasses nearby, then hopefully slung the two empty canteens over his shoulder and began to climb in the failing evening light.

He heard a flurry of movement as he reached the tank.

Softly padded footfalls, not hooves, so likely he had frightened away a coyote come to the water before its nocturnal hunting.

There was a path of sorts, probably a game trail, leading up the side of the chute above the tank. It was steep and would be difficult to traverse in the poor light.

But he was getting thirsty, and the sight of all that cool, clear, inviting water in the tank did nothing to slake his thirst. The little water remaining in the canteen down below had to be reserved for the horse. Its needs came ahead of his.

He bypassed the tank, glancing once regretfully toward the seep that was flowing slowly but steadily out from under the rocks into the suspect tank. That water should be fresh and good if he was guessing correctly, but it was also too shallow a flow to be able to capture unless he resorted to blotting it up with a rag and squeezing the result into his canteens. He would do that if it came down to it, but he would rather not.

The canteens slung on his shoulders bumped and banged against the rocks as he found handholds and began the climb above the tank.

Once he got above the massive rocks that stood above the tank the path became almost possible for a human to follow without having to cling to handholds. Bad as it was there, it was an improvement, and he was pleased with it.

The bottom of the chute was dusty-dry and rocky. Apparently the water was following under or through the rock itself here.

Longarm continued to climb, having to move mostly by feel now as the last of the daylight faded.

He found a tiny basin in a flat rock lying in the chute. The basin held water, no more than a few cups of it, but water nonetheless. Longarm bent and tasted it. There was no hint of garlic, no sweetness. There was not enough here to fill a canteen, but it was enough for him to drink. Enough to get his thoughts off his own thirst.

He knew damned good and well that he was only so desperately thirsty because he was not carrying enough water with him. He had had plenty to drink in town at lunchtime. So it was thought rather than fact that bothered him. Knowing that, though, had not made him feel any less thirsty. Now, with the clean water from the tiny basin still on his tongue, he felt better.

The jagged spires and boulders of the mountainside were honeycombed with holes and niches and small cave openings. He heard a faint sound from one of them, then a high-pitched squeal. Longarm's Colt was already in his hand and cocked before he realized it was only a bat emerging into the cool, evening sky.

"For God's sake, man, don't shoot. Don't you go and shoot ole Joe, mister. Please don't shoot."

Longarm stood with the gun in his hand, looking to both sides and up and down. He had heard the voice, but he had no idea who the hell it was he was not supposed to shoot. He could see no one in the dusk shadows.

Chapter 10

An old man, trembling and thoroughly cowed, stepped into sight on a ledge a dozen feet above Longarm.

It was a good thing he moved out where he could be easily seen. Otherwise Longarm was not sure he could have found the old fossil, even knowing the man was there and hearing his voice. The light was that bad and the hiding places that many. Longarm shoved the Colt back into his holster and climbed up to the ledge beside the man.

The fellow was a sight. Graying hair, tangled and greasy, hung halfway down his back, well below his shoulders. An equally unkempt beard matched that length on his chest. He was wild-eyed and skinny.

His clothes were mere rags: a tattered remnant of a shirt, a pair of kneeless twill trousers held up by a scrap of rope, no hat, no shoes, certainly no weapons of any sort.

It was obvious that the old boy hadn't seen a barber in

years. He smelled like he hadn't had a bath since the last time he got a haircut.

He cringed away, huddling against the rock, when Longarm reached him.

"You aren't going to shoot ole Joe, are you, mister?"

"No," Longarm said gently. "I won't hurt ole Joe." He reached forward, intending to touch the old man on the arm to reassure him, but the man flinched away from the contact.

"Are you all right?" Longarm asked. "Are you lost? Hungry? I have some food down at my camp."

The old man straightened a little at the word "food," and he took on a cunning look. "Peaches, mister? You got any peaches for ole Joe?"

"I don't have any peaches with me, Joe, but I have some dried apples and some jerky. Would you like some dried apples?"

"No peaches?" He sounded ready to cry.

"Just apples," Longarm said softly.

Joe cackled and smacked his lips. "Ole Joe likes apples."

"We'll go down to my camp, Joe. You can have your apples there." Longarm smiled at him. This time Joe allowed Longarm to touch him lightly on the elbow.

"Is there anything you want me to carry down for you?" Longarm bent toward the hole in the rock where Joe apparently had been hiding.

The old fellow acted like he was about to have a fit.

"No!" He flung himself forward, arms and legs spread wide, guarding the entrance to the narrow cave with his scrawny body. "No, mister. That's ole Joe's private place. Private. It's all the home ole Joe has. Private." He did start to cry then, large tears rolling down his wrinkled cheeks to disappear into his beard.

"All right," Longarm said patiently. "I only want to

95

help. It's all right now, Joe. I won't go in ole Joe's private place."

"You want to rob ole Joe's only home," the old boy accused.

"No," Longarm said gently. "I won't rob old Joe."

Joe gave him a suspicious look. "Double-dog promise and hope to die?" He blinked. The tears slowed their flow.

"I promise."

The old crazy man cackled happily. "You really got peaches?"

"Apples," Longarm corrected him.

"Ole Joe likes peaches better."

"I know you do, Joe. But let's go down now and get you some apples."

Old Joe giggled and danced a little jig there on the rocky ledge in front of his cave. "Ole Joe likes peaches best."

Longarm made his way back down to the chute and found the path by feel. The moon was not yet up, and it was dark as the shades of Hell.

He expected to have trouble helping old Joe down with him, but the crazy old bastard moved with the agility of a mountain goat, hopping lightly from one boulder to the next, following the hidden path as naturally as if he had lived with it for years.

Come to think of it, Longarm realized, maybe he had at that.

And if he had, by damn, it was just possible that this aging lunatic had seen whoever poisoned the Cottonwood water supply.

Lord knew, the old fool was capable of watching without being seen. The poisoners might well have been observed without their knowing it.

Toward the end of the climb, on the steep portion just above the tank, Longarm found old Joe helping *him* find the hand- and footholds. It was damn near embarrassing.

They reached the bottom eventually, and Longarm

headed past the tank. Ole Joe was no longer beside him.

Longarm turned and saw by the thin starlight that the old man was kneeling beside the tank, bending to it to drink.

"No," Longarm snapped. He jumped forward and grabbed Joe by the arm to yank him away from the fouled water. The sudden movement scared the old boy, and he began to cry again.

"Ole Joe just wants a drink, mister. That's all. Just a little drink of water."

"Not that water, Joe," Longarm explained patiently. "That water is no good. I have some good water at my camp. I'll give you a drink there. And your peaches. I mean apples, damn it. You can have a drink there, and some dried apples too."

"No water?" Joe asked plaintively.

"At the camp. Not this water."

"There is water here."

"This water is no good." Longarm considered trying to explain the problem to the old fellow. But hell, he would never be able to comprehend it. "Wait," Longarm said sternly.

Old Joe whimpered a little, but he was not crying now. He allowed Longarm to lead him the rest of the way down to the camp.

At camp Longarm got out his one remaining canteen. It was only partially full. Joe gulped at it so greedily that Longarm was sure there would be nothing left for the horse in the morning. Longarm had already resigned himself to going without water for a while, but he had not counted on this.

When Longarm dragged out the food, Joe was just as eager as he had been with the water. He ate all the dried apples and most of the jerky Longarm was carrying.

Longarm muttered a little under his breath. He was going to have to resupply damned soon or spend some hungry time. At least the old man couldn't eat the horse's graze.

The things Longarm had bought in town were for the most part back at the reservation in the guest house along with the carpetbag and other articles that Longarm had thought unnecessarily heavy to ask the brown to carry. He had not expected to be on an extended search at the time, of course. He should have known better than to make any assumptions. You would think a fellow would learn, but some things a fellow just never seemed to anticipate.

Longarm nibbled at a little of the jerky and allowed the poor, miserable old man his head. He didn't have the heart to slow a hungry man's eating.

Slowly and gently while Joe ate, Longarm tried to get him into a conversation about the water tank and who might have come there within the past month or so.

Joe mostly just sat and stuffed his mouth, barely taking time to chew before he swallowed. He must have been half-starved.

"Ole Joe doesn't see anything," he said at one point. "Ole Joe doesn't say anything." He cackled loudly and sounded proud of himself. "Ole Joe doesn't hurt anybody." He stopped abruptly, suddenly wide-eyed and fearful again. "You won't hurt ole Joe, will you mister?"

"No," Longarm assured him. "I won't hurt old Joe."

Joe seemed to consider that for a brief moment. Then he nodded once and went back to stuffing his face.

When he had eaten everything he could hold, Joe stood.

He stood there silent and motionless for a moment, staring down at Longarm, who was hunkered beside a small fire.

Without a word, Joe turned and walked away into the night.

Longarm thought he was just moving away from the campfire to relieve himself. But that took only moments, and the moment turned into minutes, and gradually Longarm realized that the old son of a bitch had gone and wandered off into the night.

He had disappeared completely, and Longarm had never heard him go.

Damn! Longarm told himself. A crazy old man, alone out here like that, could hurt himself. Fall down a damn cliff. Run afoul of a mountain cat. Almost anything. Where did he find food? Hell, he might stop and have a drink of that arsenated water on his way back up the chute. Anything could happen to him.

After a while Longarm calmed down about it. Whoever old Joe was, he must have been up here in the rocks for a long time already. He had survived so far without Longarm's help. And Longarm hadn't been given the old crazy man to raise. Old Joe was not his responsibility.

Longarm told himself that sternly over and over. Even so, he felt uneasy about the poor old man.

No, he hadn't been given old Joe to raise. But Longarm felt sorry for him and at least partially responsible for him now too.

Damn the old bastard to hell anyway.

Eventually Longarm managed to quit worrying about crazy Joe long enough to wrap up in a blanket and go to sleep, thirsty and with his belly nearly empty.

Tomorrow would look better.

It almost had to.

He found another slow seep up on top of the mountain in the morning. It was a hell of a climb getting up there, but there was water enough to let the horse drink its fill, replenish all three canteens, and have a long, damned welcome drink for himself too. Longarm felt better after that.

He turned the horse downhill again. In spite of all his good intentions, he had wakened this morning worrying about that stinking—he really did stink, too—old Joe. He wasn't going to feel right about the old boy until he checked to make sure Joe was safely "home."

It was a bit of a trick finding his way back to the chute from the top of the thing. The country was so rugged here, so rock-cut and ragged, that ten feet of movement made the whole world take on a different shape, or so it seemed.

Longarm kept at it until he was at the top of the chute, though, then tied the horse to the twisted trunk of a runty juniper growing out of a crack in the rock and made his way carefully down.

The ledge where he had seen Joe—all right, the ledge where Joe had seen *him*—was right up there. He thought. It had been nearly dark then, and he had been coming from a different direction.

He checked the ground for footprints. Something of a trick on hard rock, but he did find some indentations in the gravel here and there that could have been footprints. He was fairly sure.

He climbed up to the ledge and was convinced that that was the way he had come the night before.

"Joe? Are you in there, Joe?"

There was no answer. A bird flitted past overhead, going down toward the water tank. The thing was sure to die if it drank there.

"Joe?"

Silence was the only answer he received.

He was positive, though, that the narrow cave opening in front of him was Joe's private place. It almost had to be.

Longarm had promised he would not disturb old Joe's home. But, hell, he wasn't going to bother anything. He just wanted to satisfy himself that Joe had made it back up in the dark last night. Surely there could not be anything wrong with that.

He went into the cave. The opening was narrow, his body blocking out the light as he stood at the entrance. He moved forward, feeling his way along, careful not to bash his head against the ceiling.

The passage became wider as he went deeper into the cave, allowing more light to filter past him. Even so, the deeper he went the less light could reach inside. He struck a match and held it in front of him.

There was nothing.

The cave petered out twenty-five or thirty feet into the rock. The floor of the open area was lightly covered with coarse sand, and at the far back and there there was a pool of water puddled against the rock wall.

But there was no sign of Joe.

The old fellow had disappeared.

The first match burned down to his fingers, and Longarm dropped it with a curse and lighted another.

There was sign aplenty that someone had occupied the cave at one time, although just how recently would have been impossible to determine. With neither wind nor weather to disturb the sandy floor, the vague footprints could have been left behind by Joe last night or by some ancient-history Indian a thousand years ago. There was no way to tell.

Over against the right wall was a pile of dry wood, cedar and juniper and even some cottonwood limbs that had been broken into faggot lengths and carried in here.

On the left was a flat, compressed area where a bed had been laid. There was no bed there now, though, and no Ole Joe.

"Damn," Longarm said aloud. The sound echoed back from the tone and reverberated around his head.

There was only the firewood, the place where a bed had been, and the pool of water.

Longarm raised an eyebrow and went forward to kneel beside the pool. The second match went out, so he dropped it and found the water by feel. There would be light enough toward the opening to find his way back out again, and he had already seen everything there was to see in this crude habitation.

He cupped water into his palm and raised it, smelling of it before he tasted it. Here again there was no smell of garlic and no flavor. The water was fresh and sweet.

Yet Joe had been thirsty as hell when he got down to the camp last night. It made no sense. But then, Longarm reflected, nothing about that poor old halfwit made any sense anyway. There was no point worrying about it.

He took one last look around in the dim interior of the cave. His eyes were beginning to adjust to the darkness, so he could see a little anyhow.

Joe had sure been insistent about his privacy, but there was damn sure nothing here to be private about. Not unless the old fellow was possessive about a few hundredweight of gravelly sand and a puddle of fresh water.

Longarm shrugged. For all he knew, Joe *was* that crazily possessive.

Or, then again, the old fellow could have come back up to the cave and cleared out of it once he was discovered.

Longarm struck another match and went over to where the bed had been. He found a few threads of burlap snagged against the stone. So the bed hadn't been made by some ancient Indian. It had to have been Joe's. Now it was empty. The old man had moved on.

Longarm felt no regret for the time he had lost here. He felt better knowing that Joe must have made it home last night.

He felt a bit sad to think that his accidental presence had frightened the old fellow into new quarters, but there were more than enough caves to go around in this swiss-cheese mountain country.

Besides, maybe his new location would be someplace where people could keep an eye on him, make sure he had something to eat now and then, check on him occasionally to make sure he wasn't laid up sick or with a broken leg or something and unable to take care of himself. Longarm decided he would talk to the Ka-Ays about it, see if they would be willing to keep an eye out for the old fellow.

He made his way back out of the cave, blinking and squinting in the bright daylight after the interior of the cave, and back up to the horse.

Damn that old fellow, anyway. Longarm had work to do, and chasing after a mad hermit wasn't getting any of it done.

By now those folks back in Cottonwood would likely be groaning about having to drive all the way down to the Pecos for their drinking water.

Longarm just hoped James Morrison could hold the line down there while Longarm took care of the rest of this job.

Chapter 11

This might be it. These might be the men he wanted up here. They certainly looked the part. Shaggy, greasy, ugly sons of bitches, coming up from the south on one of the myriad narrow trails with a string of loaded pack mules.

Bringing more poison? Longarm wondered.

Could be. He had talked that over with James. According to the sketchy information they had been able to gather from James's books and some educated guessing on the part of the schoolmaster, it would have taken tons of the low-grade arsenate poison to contaminate the water supply of Cottonwood so thoroughly. Certainly it was not the sort of poison a man could carry in a hip pocket flask to dump into a well.

So these could be his suspects coming right to him.

Longarm eased the brown horse behind a squat tower of gray rock and dismounted, pulling the Winchester from its scabbard. He clambered onto the broad top of the barn-sized boulder and lay there, shading his eyes and trying to get a better look at the men who were approaching, unaware of his presence.

There were two of them, dusty and sitting heavy in their saddles from long travel. Coming from that direction, they might have been coming up from El Paso.

Heading for the tank to dump in more arsenates? There was no way to know at the moment. But an examination of the packs on those seven mules would tell the story. If the wooden crates lashed on each side of the packframes held powders that smelled like garlic, Longarm would have reason for some real serious questioning.

The two men had not spotted him so far. He was sure of that. And their line of travel should take them within a dozen feet of his hiding place. The thing to do would be to wait until they were close, then confront them.

If they were innocent travelers with nothing to hide, no harm would be done. But on the other hand . . .

He shifted the Winchester a little closer to hand. Already the sun had heated the blued-steel action until it was uncomfortably warm to the touch. He adjusted the set of his hat to shade the side of his face from the bite of the harsh sun.

The men and horses and mules plodded forward, moving with the slow, monotonous pace of long travel. Wherever these men had come from, whatever they were doing here, they were not locals out for a morning's work. The loads in those crates were heavy, too. Even moving as slowly as they were, the mules were caked with drying sweat-lather, salt crusted where the sweat of their labors quickly dried in the hot air of these desert mountains. That would be consistent with the dead bulk of arsenate powders, Longarm thought. He grunted softly to himself and checked his pockets to make sure he had a ready supply of loose ammunition if he needed to reload in a hurry. He did. He nearly always did. But strong habit made him verify that, even knowing full well that he did.

"Just a little closer," Longarm whispered to himself.

One of the men, the one in the lead, reined his mount out of the path and stopped. Longarm's head rose a fraction of an inch and his eyes narrowed. If they had seen him . . .

They had not. The man paused only long enough for his partner to reach his side. He said something and pointed to the north. The second man nodded agreement, and the train plodded forward again.

That water tank was to the north. Were they pointing toward it? Were they pleased that they were near their destination and could do their murderous work against women and infants and disappear into the south again?

Possible, of course.

Damn it. Damn whoever had been doing this. What reason could there be? It was a question Longarm had been asking himself all morning. What reason could there be for anyone to poison a town's water supply?

There had to be one. No one goes to that kind of trouble without almighty good reason for his labors.

Surely even the most evil of men must have powerful justification for the killing of babes in arms.

Even the kind of low-life son of a bitch who takes pleasure in killing or in the pain of others would surely not choose poisoning as his method. Surely that kind would want to be present to see the results of his deeds. Certainly all of the crazy people—a much worse kind of crazy than poor old Joe the hermit—that Longarm had known in the past had been that way. None of them, no matter how vile a human being, would have poisoned children to death and not made any effort to watch the suffering.

Longarm damn sure hoped these two men here could tell him the truth of this phony curse bullshit.

The train moved closer. They were forty yards away

now and eighteen, twenty feet below the rock-top level where Longarm lay waiting for them.

Another twenty yards, he thought. Close enough that the threat of his Winchester would intimidate them. Far enought still that they would not want to risk the inaccuracies of revolver fire. Both carried rifles on their saddles, but the rifles were in saddle scabbards and would be slow to reach. He wanted them positioned so that they would not be tempted to fight, so that he had the upper hand and could get a look into those crates with the least possible trouble.

Another fifteen yards . . .

Behind and below him the brown horse nickered a welcome to the animals in the pack train.

Hell, Longarm muttered. They were tipped. They had to have heard.

Innocent travelers in this empty, rugged country could have been expected to react, to prepare to defend themselves if necessary.

These men, tired and bored though they were, reacted with a speed and a deliberate purpose that caught even Longarm off guard.

They were good, damn it.

The nearer of them wheeled his horse left, dropping from the saddle as he did so and rolling behind some low rocks next to the trail.

His partner behind him whirled left and performed the same manuever, emptying his saddle and taking cover instantly.

There was no hesitation in either man. No wait for consultation or consideration. Certainly no readiness to greet another innocent traveler on the high trails.

Both men reacted with almost instinctive speed and practice.

The one thing Longarm had going for him was that neither man had time enough—or took time enough—to grab his rifle when he left the saddle. Both were armed only with short weapons.

"Hold it!" Longarm called loudly. "No need to get excited. I just want to talk to you." He knew better than to rise up and expose himself, though. He spoke to them from the protection of the solid stone where he was lying.

"Talk about what?" one of them called. Neither of them was willing to expose himself either.

Longarm took a deep breath. If they were not lawful travelers in this country...

"Federal officer investigating a crime," he shouted. "I just want to have word with you, peaceable, and take a look in those packs."

"All right. Give us a look at you, federal man."

"Go easy," Longarm called back.

"We just want to look at you. Make sure you ain't gunning for us or tryin' to rob us."

"Easy now."

Instead of rising to his knees and showing himself, Longarm shifted to the side a few feet, took off his hat, and shoved it forward at the point where he had just been, using the muzzle of his Winchester to slide it across the gritty rock. It was an old dodge, and an effective one.

The flat, dull report of a large-caliber revolver sounded, quickly followed by a second as both men fired at what they thought was the federal officer's head.

So much for these two being innocent travelers in a hard land.

One slug missed entirely, cutting a bee-drone path through the air close enough for Longarm to hear. The other slashed wickedly across the surface of the boulder, sending a spray of rock chips over Longarm and ticking the brim of the Stetson to spin it high into the air.

Longarm considered playing possum, but these two were too good to think they had come away that easily. They would know where their shots had gone.

"Damn you, boys. That was a good hat," he shouted.

"You won't mind for long," one of them promised him.

They did seem to want this done the hard way, then.

Longarm thought the voice reached him from a slightly different angle. So they were moving. And they were good. These two worked well together. It was time, he thought, to do something about them.

He shifted backward again, came to his knees once he was well behind the protection of the boulder, and crabbed over to the side of the barn-sized rock until he could drop down to more or less level ground again.

One of them was in position to get a glimpse of him as he came off the rock. Again there was the report of a gunshot, and stone chips stung his cheek and shoulder. If this kept up, Longarm was going to get pissed.

He crouched in the shelter of the boulder, then hefted the Winchester, got down on his belly, and skinned forward to lie underneath a damned thorny bush.

Deputy Long was the one on the defensive now, damn that horse.

"Now," a voice said softly from somewhere on the other side of the huge boulder.

The number two man rose up from the rocks not a dozen feet in front of Longarm and charged forward with his pistol at the ready.

Longarm had no choice about it. He triggered a flat-nosed slug into the man's chest. The impact of it ripped through the man's breastbone, stopping him in his tracks and dropping him like a poleaxed shoat.

Longarm did not have to look for the other one. He knew where the man had to be. This was a coordinated attack from two directions. And his long-barreled, awkward Winchester was pointed in the wrong damn direction.

The other one would be counting on that. And counting too on a man not abandoning a weapon he already had in his hands.

Longarm dropped the Winchester and rolled onto his back, his hand sweeping the Colt out even as he moved and pointing it past his feet as he lay there on the hard ground.

The remaining gunman burst into view around the back of the boulder almost before his dead partner had time to hit the ground, revolver cocked and leveled and a grim, satisfied smile already on him.

Not this time.

Longarm's finger tightened on the trigger of the double-action Colt, and the gun bucked in his fist.

The bullet took the man high on the right side of his chest and spun him sideways. He lost his balance and toppled forward. But he was still alive, and still had his revolver.

"Drop it," Longarm said.

The man was on his knees, head down, the shock and pain of the wound pulling his features into a pale, haggard mask. His right hand and arm seemed to be useless, probably numbed by the impact of the slug. He let go of it and picked it up with his left.

"Drop it," Longarm said again.

"Go to hell," the gunman snarled.

With a wild-eyed glare of hate and determination, he tried it. Wounded and hurting and left-handed, he nevertheless tried it. The gun barrel came up, and he fumbled for the hammer.

Longarm shot him again.

"Damn it," Longarm muttered. "I wanted to talk to you." If it would have been possible he might have shot to disable and not kill. But when there are real bullets in the other man's gun that would be a fool's play. If you have time enough to take careful aim, you probably don't need to shoot at all. Longarm's .45 slug ripped through the man's left temple, rearranging the shape of his head.

110

There would be no information out of this one.

Longarm went back to check the other man. Carefully. The shot had looked like a killing one, but Longarm was not willing to bet his life on that.

It was a bet he would have gotten away with this time. The second man was dead too, lying face forward in a puddle of bright blood.

"Well, shit," Longarm said to no one.

He retrieved his Winchester and reloaded both rifle and revolver, then walked out of the shelter of the boulders.

Both saddle horses were standing placidly cropping grass despite the noise of the gunfire. The string of mules had tried to run but had managed to get themselves tangled when all seven chose a different direction to flee. A string of horses might have panicked and broken their own necks trying to fight the restraint of the lead ropes that linked them together, but mules were brighter than that. They had accepted the inevitable and now were nervously huddled together about seventy-five yards back down the trail.

Longarm went to them and spoke in a low, soothing tone as he got the mules calmed. When he had them sorted out he randomly picked a crate and used his knife to pry the lid free.

"Well, I will be damned," he said to himself.

These old boys hadn't been hauling poison powders to the water. But it was no wonder they hadn't wanted to stop and chat with a federal officer.

Each one of those crates, fourteen of them, one on each side of each mule's packframe, held half a dozen brand new Army-issue Springfield carbines, model of 1873 breachloaders in .45-70 caliber.

The Springfield Armory government markings were stamped clear and bold on their receivers, and the carbines were still packed in their shipping grease. The weapons had to have been stolen. There was no other explanation for them being in civilian hands. So those boys had had reason enough to get snuffy when a federal deputy wanted a word with them.

Longarm looked back toward the dead men. Lordy, but he wished he could have talked to them.

Eighty-four brand new breach-loading carbines in a caliber big enough to kill buffalo at four hundred yards.

Where were they going? Why? Who was the buyer? What the hell did he want with so many stolen carbines, and what was he going to do with them?

And could the presence of these carbines have anything to do with the poisonings in Cottonwood?

Damn, but he would have liked to be able to ask those boys some questions.

That was not possible, not this side of Hell anyway, and he could not wait that long.

Now that he had the string of mules and their loads of weaponry another question occurred to him. What the hell was he going to do with them?

He couldn't leave them here for any passing jehu to dip into. He did not want to turn them over to Agent Farady at the reservation for safekeeping. That would amount to arming the Kiowa-Apache if things came to a head over the damned curse. And, on the other side of that coin, he did not want to take them to Cottonwood either. That would be the same as arming the Texans, as good as pointing the people of Cottonwood toward the Ka-Ays and saying sic 'em.

He cussed and mumbled some, ate some jerky and hardtack he found in one of the dead men's saddlebags, and finally came up with a halfway sensible idea. But it was going to take some work, and he would get a bit greasy before he was done.

It really did not matter, though, where he stored the Springfields as long as there were no firing pins in the breachblocks.

Taking time for that sure was going to cut into an already precariously thin timetable for getting the situation here under control.

He couldn't see any way around it, though. And standing around staring was not going to get the job done. Longarm rolled up his sleeves and started pulling spanking new Springfields out of the first crate.

Chapter 12

It was well past dark by the time Longarm reached his destination. The horse could have made it in half the time, but a pack string of already tired mules cannot be hurried. The lights of Cottonwood glowed softly as he and the mules rode in. He had chosen to come here to store the Springfields simply because Cottonwood was a good dozen miles closer from the scene of the fight than the reservation would have been. And he did not want to waste any more time on this than was absolutely necessary.

"Find Ranger Sharply for me, would you, sonny?" he asked a youngster he saw outside a closed storefront.

The boy grinned and set off at a run down the street, not even waiting to ask what he would get out of it. Longarm relaxed for the first time since the fight and hooked a knee across the pommel of his saddle while he lighted a cheroot and waited for Sharply to show up.

He had had more than enough time to think about the

situation since he started pulling firing pins from the carbines—slim strips of turned metal that were now bundled and resting separately in Longarm's saddlebags—and it had occurred to him that the two men he had run into might not have been alone. There could be other gun-running pack trains on the mountain, traveling in small groups to avoid attracting attention.

The reason he suspected that was because eighty-four carbines might be enough to fight a small war with, but not without ammunition. The crates on the mules held only the Springfields. Not one round of .45-70 ammo. He had to assume that whoever was buying the carbines would be buying ammunition too.

Hell, for all Longarm knew, that unknown party might very well be stocking up with Gatling guns and mountain howitzers too. He had intercepted one shipment of weapons. That did not mean there were not others.

Sharply and Junior came up the street following the boy Longarm had sent for them. The Ranger's eyes narrowed when he saw who wanted him. The boy must not have told him that.

Longarm gave the kid a dime and sent him on his way.

"I see you're packed," Sharply said drily, eyes drifting toward the loaded pack mules behind the brown. "Fixing to leave the country, are you?" As usual Junior said nothing, content to follow his father's lead. Neither of them mentioned Longarm giving them the slip at the schoolhouse the day before.

"We're supposed to be cooperating, aren't we?" Longarm asked.

"What's that mean?"

"I have some government property here. Thought I'd best turn it over to competent local authority for safekeeping."

"Yeah?"

Longarm explained the situation to him. Some of it,

anyway. He did not bother to mention the fact that the Springfields had been disabled. If things happened to get out of hand around Cottonwood, well, he would as soon have the battles fought with useless weapons as with good ones. Not that he expected that to happen, but there was no point in taking chances.

"Well, I'll be damned," Sharply said.

"Could be." Longarm drew on his cheroot and tossed the butt down into the dirt of the street. "The question is, would you put these government arms into storage until the army can send a detail to take possession of them?"

"I expect I could do that."

"Good."

"Where'd you say the . . . uh . . . thieves were bound?" It was occurring to him, as Longarm had expected it would, that the weapons could have been destined for the Kiowa-Apache reservation if the Indians too were preparing for a fight.

"Naturally they didn't make me a party to their plans," Longarm said. "We were a mite too busy for that. But what I'd guess from the way they were headed was that they were taking the guns south. Likely figuring to sell them to the next would-be *presidente* of all Mexico. But of course that's just a guess."

"Headed south, huh?"

"That's right," Longarm lied.

Sharply grunted. He scratched under his chin for a moment, then turned to Junior. "Son, take these critters off the deputy's hands now. Lead 'em down to the gunsmith's. I believe Conrad has a basement where we can put 'em, and I'm sure he'll let us use it." To Longarm he said, "Secure storage that way. It's where Conrad stores all his powder an' valuable weapons."

"That sounds all right to me." Longarm handed the lead rope to Junior, and the younger Sharply set off down the street with the weary mules following him. "I'll get my

116

report off to Fort Davis by mail. Can't tell you when they'll send somebody to fetch the guns."

"They'll be safe until," Sharply said.

"Then I'll be on my way. Thanks for your help, Ranger. It's always nice to have the cooperation of the local authorities." Longarm said it with a straight face.

"Anything I can do t' help, federal man. But then, I expect you already knew that."

"I never had a doubt of it, Ranger." Longarm nodded and turned the brown away.

He rode west out of town, back toward the mountains, although he had no intention of pushing the brown that far tonight. He just wanted to make sure Ned Sharply would not be worried about Deputy Longarm's whereabouts in Cottonwood.

Once he was well clear of the town lights he pulled off the road and dismounted to smoke another cigar, listening to the night sounds more than trying to see into the darkness. No one was following him. He took his time and made sure of it.

Then he remounted and rode back toward the small adobe house at the western edge of Cottonwood. He wanted to have a word with Morrison and see how the schoolmaster's deception was going.

Longarm left the horse hobbled and turned free to graze in a shallow swale southwest of Cottonwood and across the creekbed, where it was unlikely to be discovered. He walked the rest of the way, approaching the house Meaghan Morrison had described as her brother's from the rear so he would not be seen.

He moved silently through the shadows.

That turned out to be a mistake.

He naturally came to the kitchen door, intending to knock softly for entry. Instead he stood where he was, knowing he should turn away, but rooted to the spot.

Meaghan Morrison was in the kitchen. With no idea in

the world that anyone could be watching, she was just finishing a bath.

As Longarm could all too clearly see, she was in the process of stepping out of a zinc-lined tub to dry herself.

Lord, but that lovely young woman did have herself a figure to match the rest of her appearance.

Sleek and shiny with dripping bath water, as if her pale flesh had been polished and highlighted in the lamplight, she was full-busted and flat-bellied.

Her hair was done up with pins to keep it from becoming damp. The effect was to make prominent the slender, corded column of her neck and to emphasize the delicate outlines of her collarbone and throat.

Longarm felt himself growing hard. He had to shift himself under the restraint of his trousers.

Meaghan's body was slim. He could see the pattern of her ribcage and the sharp projections of her pelvic bones on either side of a short, curling bush of pubic hair.

He stood where he was and watched as she toweled herself dry from the bath and reached up to unpin her hair.

The movement of her arms tightened and raised her breasts, tilting them toward the ceiling. Her breasts were not overlarge, but they were full and unusually firm, with small, dark, sharp-tipped nipples.

He probably had seen women who were more desirable than Meg Morrison. Right now he was not particularly interested in remembering when that might have been.

She finished drying, wiping herself carefully between the thighs and in the crack of her deliciously rounded bottom. She tossed her head, sending her hair cascading over her shoulders and down onto the slopes of her breasts.

There was an oversized robe draped on a chair nearby —probably James's—but she did not reach for it immediately. First she opened a small leather case and took out several vials and a box of scented powder. She powdered her body, a faint smile on her lips as she did so, then opened one of the vials and applied a touch of scent under each ear, another in the hollow of her throat, more beneath her breasts, finally a brief application of the perfume on either side of her sex.

Longarm damn near groaned. The thought of that body entwined with his . . .

It occurred to him that this was Saturday night. She was expecting him to call this weekend. They had discussed that back at her schoolhouse on the reservation days ago. He had forgotten about that until this moment. The original idea had been for her to introduce him to her brother, but of course that was no longer necessary.

He had forgotten, but she must not have. It seemed entirely possible that she was preparing herself for his visit, that her interest had been stronger than he suspected before.

He felt a weighty throb of desire for Meg Morrison. It wouldn't do, though, for her to know that he had seen those preparations. He should have turned away from the back of the house as soon as he realized what was going on. He just hadn't been able to do what he knew damn good and well he should have.

So he stayed where he was, silent and motionless at the back of the house, until Meg Morrison finished with her toilet, pulled on the too-large robe—he thought she looked almighty fetching in the thick folds of cloth with the sleeves rolled up—and went out of his sight into the front of the house.

His desire for her was so strong it was approaching the point of pain. He had to take long, deliberate, steadying breaths and will himself sternly to back off. He was, after all, calling on her brother.

Of course, if anything else should happen to occur . . .

He waited a good five minutes before he tapped lightly on the doorframe. When he did it was James who answered.

James too was dressed for bed. He smiled when he saw who the late-night caller was. Longarm doubted James would have been so pleasant if he knew of Longarm's interest in his sister. But of course he could not.

"Could I come insde, James? I don't want to be seen here."

"Of course." James let him in and turned down the wick of one lamp in the kitchen and extinguished the others. They sat in the kitchen to talk. Meaghan did not join them.

Longarm found himself thinking about her rather than his mission here. She could be shy, in spite of the preparations. She could very well expect to be courted. For whatever reason, she remained in the front of the house except to give him a brief, restrained greeting when James told her who their guest was.

James's report was optimistic. He had made up a likely-sounding disease, creating it from whole cloth, lengthy Latin name and all, to insure against anyone else in town finding the signs and symptoms of a real disease in their own medical encyclopedia and disputing James's claims about the drinking water.

The townspeople were accepting his warnings for the time being and had organized a volunteer force to take turns hauling barrels of drinking water from the Pecos by wagon.

One more child had come down with signs of arsenate poisoning, but the youngster who had already been sick and expected to die by the week's end was alive still and responding to the treatments James prescribed for his non-existent disease.

The treatment called for broths and hot compresses and bed rest along with daily applications of sugar-whiskey toddies. That could do no harm, James explained, and it gave people something concrete to do about the "disease." The real treatment, of course, was a cessation of intake of

the arsenates, which were cumulative in effect, each suc-
ceeding drink of water building the level of posions in the
ailing children's systems.

"You've done damned well," Longarm said. He meant
it. Without James Morrison and his imaginary disease the
town of Cottonwood and the reservation Kiowa-Apache
would already be at war. The man was giving Longarm no
guarantees, but he was certainly presenting the federal deputy with an opportunity to avert disaster and bloodshed
here.

"What about Sharply and his shoot-'em-up crowd?"
Longarm asked.

"They're skeptical. Ned as much as asked if your visit
the other day had anything to do with my disease reports.
But he hasn't actually accused me of anything. The Tre-
mayne child still being alive and beginning to respond to
my so-called treatments has been the biggest thing in our
favor. People will find it difficult to reject what I am telling
them if they see that sort of positive result from following
my advice."

"And, of course, if the parents don't give the child any
more tainted water, she should recover."

"I hope so. Lord God, Longarm, I don't know anything
about medicine, though. I keep thinking that a real doctor
might be able to do something to remove the poisons from
our systems. We all carry it, of course. Every one of us
who has been drinking well water. And that means all of
us. There could be long-term effects of the poisons that
could be dealt with if people knew the truth, but that could
go unrealized this way."

"Would a doctor come if you sent for one?"

"I think so."

"I need a little more time, James, but it isn't my intention to wipe out the town of Cottonwood. Not hardly. Just
as quick as we get to the bottom of this poisoning business,

121

we'll call in a physician. I think I can get an army doctor sent here if need be. But I don't want anyone to know quite yet. I still need time, James."

"That makes me feel better, Longarm. Much better."

"Good. Oh . . . could I borrow some writing paper and a pen from you? I need to post a report to Fort Davis about some recovered government property. You could mail it for me if you would."

"Anything I can do." Morrison went into the front of the house and returned a moment later with a folio for writing paper, pens, and dried ink that he mixed for Longarm.

"Does your sister know the truth about the poisonings?" Longarm asked.

"Yes. I keep no secrets from Meaghan, Longarm. But she'll not give it away. She promised to say nothing to anyone at the reservation."

"All right." Longarm was hoping to use that as an excuse to talk with Meg Morrison this evening, but she seemed to have gotten a bad case of the shies at the last moment. And he couldn't come right out and ask James if it would be all right to see his sister so he could take a crack at getting into her drawers. That wouldn't go over particularly well.

Longarm wrote out his report and addressed it to the commander of the garrison at Fort Davis, Texas. He thought Davis was closer than Sumner, and there should be regular troops there instead of the Remount people to the north.

"That should do it," he said once the envelope was sealed and he had given James change for a stamp.

"I would invite you to stay, Longarm, but with Meaghan here there isn't any extra room."

That had been his last hope for an excuse to spend some time with Meg Morrison tonight.

"Of course, James. I wouldn't think of putting you out."

Like hell he wouldn't. Put old James out and put it in Meg if he ever got half a chance.

"Oh, I almost forgot," he said, grasping at straws so he could stay a bit longer in the hope that something might turn up. "Do you know anything about a crazy old man living in the mountains? He calls himself Joe."

James smiled. "We all know about Mad Joe. They tell me he showed up a year or so back. Quite a lunatic, I hear. Have you met him?"

Longarm nodded.

"I certainly envy you, then. I would give anything to be able to talk to him."

"Whatever for? He's just an old madman."

Morrison snorted. "Now he is, or so they tell me. But not in his day."

"It'd be hard to believe that the poor old thing ever had himself a day."

"To the contrary, Longarm, he once was quite the gentleman."

"Crazy Joe?" That sounded far-fetched in the extreme.

"Oh, yes. His name is, or was, I suppose one might have to say now, Joseph F. Franklyn. He was quite famous in his time. The man with the golden touch."

"Never heard of him," Longarm said.

"Perhaps not. You probably had no reason to. For Meaghan and I, well there is a personal reason why we would remember him." Morrison leaned back in his chair and his eyes took on a faraway look.

"Meaghan and I came from Baltimore, you see. Our father . . . was in business there. Joseph Franklyn was his idol. Franklyn was the leading financer of the city during the War. He made his fortune buying Southern cotton out of northern Mexico and shipping it to England, France, and Holland for sale. I don't suppose it was very patriotic of him, but it certainly earned him his fortune almost over-

123

night. After the War he invested in other ventures. Like I said, he was the man with the golden touch. Whatever he turned his hand to prospered. That was until the great market crash of seventy-two." Morrison shook his head.

"Our father was wiped out in that same crash." His smile was bitter. "We have good reason to remember it, you see."

"Of course."

Morrison shrugged. "I suppose Joseph Franklyn came out of it better than our father did. He lived. Went mad as a hatter, of course, but he lived. Our father . . . shot himself in the downstairs study. Meaghan and I were in her room playing a game of some sort. I remember the sound of the gunshot." He shuddered. The memory seemed difficult for him even after the passage of so much time.

Then he regained control and gave Longarm a wan smile. "Silly of me." He sighed. "Anyway, I was telling you about this Mad Joe, wasn't I? After the stock market crash ruined him financially he disappeared for a time. I recall an editorial in one of the Baltimore newspapers— one that had opposed Franklyn during his Midas days— giving him the laugh because he was expecting to remake his fortunes buying buffalo hides and selling them for industrial belting. The laugh was that this was just about the time the buffalo were finally being exterminated, as the newspaper was pleased to point out for their readers. After that, well, I hadn't heard anything more about him until I learned he was supposed to be here, living a hermit's existence in the Guadalupes. As I said, though, I should like to be able to talk with him. I keep thinking . . . oh, I don't know . . . that his experiences might give me some insight into my father's despair, or . . . I can't really say, I just would like to meet him."

"Perhaps you'll have a chance someday," Longarm said softly. "Although I suspect you would be disappointed. He isn't Joseph Franklyn any more. Just Mad Joe. Living in his own world somewhere that the rest of us can't reach him."

"Could it be that my father had the better of it, Longarm?"

"That's one I couldn't answer for you, James."

Morrison sighed heavily.

"I'd best be going now, James." After this, Longarm's mood wasn't bent on seduction any longer.

"Yes. Good night, Longarm." James did not look up or stand as Longarm let himself out the back door and sneaked back toward the waiting horse.

Tonight's camp promised to be an unusually lonely one with shy Meg Morrison back there in the adobe house and James brooding near her. Longarm knew damn good and well he would not be getting much sleep for thinking about all the promise of that sleek, fine body alone in a bed not so very far away.

Damn it all, anyhow.

Chapter 13

The trail Longarm was following steepened, the brown's iron-shod hooves slipping on the bare rock for lack of purchase. The horse shook its head in annoyance and pinned its ears, then gathered itself and lunged forward in a scramble. Longarm leaned over its withers so his weight would not interfere, and the horse burst forward to the top of the incline and over it.

Longarm pulled the animal to a stop and reached for his Colt. The last upward scramble had carried him smack into the middle of a group of men sitting around a late breakfast fire, although it must have been eight or nine o'clock in the morning.

The men smiled at him and waved, and he relaxed a little. The horse was panting under him and trembling a little after the hard exertion of the climb.

"Come. Join us," one of the men invited.

Longarm stepped off the brown and loosened his cinch.

The men were Mexicans. A dozen . . . no, more. There were sixteen of them gathered around two separate fires and seemingly in no hurry to get on with their day.

The fires were made from dried manure and a few twigs, which was why he had not spotted any smoke before he topped the grade.

His first impression, that they might be a group of bandits up from the border to hide from the Federales, had to be false. There were a few firearms to be seen in the bunch, but very few. A battered loose-powder Sharps here, and old musket with half the barrel cut away over there. A scattering of handguns among them, mostly aging single shots. No, this crowd was not armed for trouble. Not with the Federales or anybody else.

Besides, they certainly looked friendly enough.

"We have beans," the first man offered. He grinned and shrugged. "They are hot. This I can say of them."

"Beans would be real welcome," Longarm told him. "And is that coffee I smell?"

The man's grin got bigger. *"Sí.* Hot enough to burn, thick enough you only need the cup to keep it from burning the hands, yes?"

"Sounds perfect. I had a piece of beef jerky and a drink of water 'long about dawn."

"Then join us, *señor."*

Longarm introduced himself and got a round of names in return. The only one he remembered for sure was Juan Cardenas, the man who had spoken first and the one who seemed to be in charge. If anyone was. They were a loose, comfortable-looking crowd. "It's my pleasure, *Señor* Cardenas." The name was pure Spanish, but Juan Cardenas looked like he had a good deal of Indio in him. His complexion was dark and his face and neck weathered, but his smile was large and his dark eyes merry.

They were a young crowd too, mostly in their twenties or late teens. Cardenas looked to be the oldest of the bunch, and Longarm doubted that he had seen thirty yet.

One of the men brought Longarm a plate heaped with pinto beans that had been cooked, mashed together, flavored with hot peppers, and re-cooked. Another man found a spare tin cup, wiped it out carefully with a forefinger that was dirtier than the cup could have been, and brought coffee for the guest.

"*Gracias*," Longarm said. He squatted on the ground near Cardenas and thoroughly enjoyed the unexpected treat of a real breakfast. The man had not lied. Both the beans and the coffee were hot enough to scald, the coffee that way from the fire and the beans from their own inner sources.

"You are here seeking bad men?" Cardenas asked when Longarm was nearly done.

He shrugged. "Here looking, mostly. Have you seen any bad men lately?"

Cardenas threw his head back and laughed, and so did most of the other men who were near. So apparently most of them spoke English pretty well. That was all right. Longarm hadn't had that much reason to use his rusty Spanish lately.

"No, *señor*. the only man we have seen in many days is a . . ." He groped for it in English, then gave up. "A *loco*. You know?"

Longarm smiled. "Old Joe. Sure, I know him."

Cardenas spread his hands. "Not so bad a man, eh?"

"No, just sad," Longarm agreed.

"Just so. We fed him beans and coffee." Cardenas chuckled. "He wanted peaches."

"That's him, all right."

"No one else, *señor*."

"Oh, well. I don't know what I'm looking for anyhow. Like I said, mostly just looking. What are you boys doing up here, if you don't mind me asking?" He would have had to admit to a good bit of curiosity about what this rather

128

large crowd of Mexicans was doing up here in the Guadalupes.

Cardenas's smile practically split his face in half. "Gold, *señor*."

Longarm raised an eyebrow and waited for the rest of the joke. It took him a moment to realize that Cardenas and his friends seemed to be serioius.

"Don't you boys know that this isn't exactly gold country? Limestone and sheep shit around here, Juan. That isn't prime gold diggings. Why, I doubt there's any ore this side of the Sangre de Cristos."

The men nearby grinned at Longarm, and a few of them snickered.

"You boys figure you know something the rest of us don't, is that it?"

Cardenas smiled happily and nodded. "From long ago my people have known this."

"From long ago," Longarm repeated. He took a swallow of the stout coffee and reached for a pair of cheroots, having to settle for offering a smoke only to Cardenas, as he hadn't enough to go around for everyone.

"Sí," Cardenas affirmed.

"Gold," Longarm said.

"Sí." Cardenas looked at him with amusement, then burst into laughter. "I know, *señor*. You think we must be the same as the loco old man to be here looking for gold. But our fathers have told us there is the legend of gold here." He shrugged and said, "In Coahuila the crops are poor and the *señoritas* weary of us. So we come here to look for the gold our fathers say must be here."

"Your fathers know these things, do they?"

Longarm was not entirely clear whether Cardenas was talking about their dads or maybe about their village priests. Not that it mattered.

"Oh, but yes, *señor*. Our people lived here many years, *many* years before they moved south."

"Here?"

"San Felipe de Avila," Cardenas said. "It was our home. Then the Apaches and the ugly ones, Comanches you call them, drove us away. We would have returned, but too late. By then the *Tejanos* had come to San Felipe. So now we have our village in Coahuila, and our fathers tell us of this country. They are sad when they speak of the things that were, and we desired to see the land our fathers owned. We would have come even if there was no gold to make us rich and make the *señoritas* take interest once again."

Longarm smiled. "Adventure is something all young men ought to find at least once, Juan."

"*Sí, señor* deputy. At least the one time in every young man's life."

"I haven't seen you down in Cott...uh, San Felipe," Longarm mentioned. "Have you been there yet?"

"Oh, yes. One time. They would take our money and sell us their goods, but we were not welcome. You know the feeling?"

"Believe me, I know the feeling."

Cardenas made a face. Then he smiled again. "It is of no matter. There was not so much to see that our fathers would have once seen. We came back late in the night to pray at the old church. That will please the people of our village. Then we come back up here." He burst into a broad grin. "And today, *señor* deputy, we may find the gold to make us rich."

His carefree tone quite clearly said that they had no real expectations of finding any legendary cache of gold, no rich, lost mines. But they were having such a fine time on their adventure that that mattered not at all.

Longarm took another swallow of the coffee. Now that it was beginning to cool it did not taste so good, but it was still welcome. He finished it and stood, brushing off the seat of his britches. He thanked Juan Cardenas and the other young men who might have lived in San Felipe de Avila if things had been different a generation ago.

"Good luck to you," he told them. "I hope you find your gold and your adventure too."

Cardenas grinned and shook his hand. "And may you find whatever it is you seek also, *señor* deputy."

Longarm snugged his cinch and got back onto the brown, which was feeling rested now and restive. With a touch of his hatbrim in salute, he headed on down the trail.

Chapter 14

Longarm had more company that afternoon, but not so pleasant this time.

He was dropping down into one of the small, grassy bowls that dotted these dry mountains and might have missed seeing the fellow if the horse had not shied and tried to sidestep wide around the place where the young man had crawled. Then Longarm saw the bare ankle and blue cloth trousers under a juniper and dismounted to investigate.

"Damn," he muttered as he saw what it was.

It was a young Kiowa-Apache, a kid not more than seventeen or eighteen. The boy was still alive, but that would not last long. Someone had worked him over with a knife. The most serious of the wounds was a slash across his belly that left gray coils of gut exposed, gritty now with sand and gravel from where he'd tried to crawl—to safety?

to comfort? or simply to crawl away from his own agony —and covered with flies and gnats.

It was the blood that the horse would have smelled and tried to bolt from. There was a lot of blood. Longarm was amazed that the boy was still breathing.

He took a kerchief and dampened it with water from his canteen and used that to wipe the youngster's face. It was small comfort to offer a dying kid, but it was the best he could do.

The boy's eyelids fluttered at the cool touch. Until then Longarm doubted that the kid had been aware that anyone was near.

His eyes were stuck shut by mucus and probably by tears as well. Longarm bathed them some more, and the boy was able to look at him.

"Long . . . Arm."

"Yes," he said gently. He was certain he had never met or seen this youngster before, but the kid recognized him.

"Cherita," the boy said, although speaking cost him a great deal of effort and more of pain. The word meant nothing to Longarm.

"Men," the boy said, struggling for speech, intent on getting it out. "Men took Cherita."

"Who's Cherita?"

"Girl." The kid blushed. There could not have been much blood left in him, but he managed to blush anyway, his already copper skin flusing still darker. "My . . . girl."

"Some men did this to you and took her?"

The kid nodded. "Took . . . horses. Took her. My job . . . guarding. My . . . fault. We were . . ." He blushed again and couldn't finish that one. Didn't have to. Longarm had been a randy teenager himself once. He knew what boys and girls liked to do in the sunshine.

"They took your horses?"

The boy nodded again.

"How many men?"

The kid was leaving fast. For a moment Longarm didn't think he had heard, that the boy was already too far gone. He had to try twice to get it out finally. "Four." It was barely a whisper. Longarm had to lean close to hear.

Four men. Shit. But they would have been slowed by the horses they had stolen. By the girl too, for that matter. Longarm doubted they would go far before they wanted to stop and have at her. They wouldn't have taken her to begin with if they didn't have that in mind.

He would have asked how long ago, but it was too late for that.

The boy's eyes were open, but they saw nothing. They never would again.

There was no time to waste on burying. Longarm settled for gathering a few quick armloads of greasewood and dry juniper. The dry wood would provide the flame, and the greasewood should give off a billow of smoke.

With luck someone would see and come to investigate.

Longarm built the fire and left the boy where he was.

He caught up the brown and began to look for tracks.

There were four shod horses—those would be the men the boy had told him about—and one mule that was either one big son of a bitch or was carrying a heavy load, and about sixteen head of loose horses. It was hard to judge how many were in the horse herd because of the nature of the rock terrain here. Fortunately, though, there were enough animals moving together that it would have been almost impossible to hide the tracks of their passage.

The men were not making any effort to hide their tracks, anyway. They had to be drunk or stupid or both. Longarm did not care which. He only wanted to reach them.

He followed for the better part of an hour, then saw the brown's head rise and its nostrils flare as it caught the scent of strange horses ahead. Longarm leaned forward and grabbed hold of its muzzle to distract it while he got down and led it back the way he had just come, until he found a secluded spot out of the wind where he could probably safely leave the animal without fear of it betraying him.

He pulled the Winchester from his scabbard and by habit checked the loads in it, then made sure he had spares in his pocket before he left the horse and went ahead on foot. This time he did not slip the cinch. He might be coming back in a hurry if any of them rabbited or if they were still moving. He expected them to be stopped by now, but he was not counting on that. He would cope with whatever they had to offer.

He did not want to show himself on the trail so he worked his way patiently into and through the rocks that covered the slopes.

Longarm grunted with both disgust and satisfaction when he got into the position he wanted.

Satisfaction for finding a perfect ambush location. Disgust with what he saw below him.

The Indian girl named Cherita was there, all right. And the sons of bitches had had time enough to get at her. She was stripped naked and lying on the ground, curled on her side with her arms drawn over her face to hide her shame.

All of the men must already have had time to take a turn with her, because they were as interested now in a jug one of them was passing as they were in the girl.

Longarm could not be sure from this distance, but the girl looked even younger than the dead boy had been.

At least this one had a chance to live to a greater age.

Longarm eased into a comfortable sitting position behind a flat, canted slab of sandstone and took a firm rest with his forearm on top of the boulder. The chamber of the Winchester was already loaded. He eased the hammer back to full cock.

"Time to get me some more, boys," one of the men

said. He stood and hitched at his belt, then began to undo the buttons of his fly. He stood over the girl to nudge her with his boot toe while he pulled his tool out of his pants.

"Open up, honey. It's lover boy ag'in."

That brought a round of coarse laughter from his pals.

Cherita tried to curl herself into a tighter ball of misery, and the rapist drew his foot back to deliver a kick to the small of her exposed back.

The kick never landed.

Longarm drew his bead and squeezed lightly on the trigger of the Winchester. The carbine rocked back against his shoulder with a satisfying bellow, and the man below and in front of him clutched his groin and spun around before falling.

Whatever he had had between his legs was gone now, torn away by a .44 caliber chunk of friction-heated lead and smashed into the ground behind him.

The particular effect of that shot was pure accident. Longarm would have sworn that that was so. He had misjudged the distance and the angle and overcompensated for a bullet's tendency to fly high on downhill shots.

It was an accident, but he did not regret it all that much.

Quickly he levered another cartridge into the chamber and called out, "The rest of you sit right where you are."

The man who had been shot screamed and began to flop back and forth on the ground.

One of the others rose and made as if to go to his wounded friend. Longarm held his fire, unwilling to shoot a man down for that.

Then the sneaky son of a bitch turned away from his pal and made a dive for cover.

Longarm shot, but too late. The bullet sprayed gravel half a step behind him.

The others took that opportunity to scurry for cover too, all of them ignoring their friend, who continued to wail out his agony.

The girl was moving too, but unlike the men she was not headed for cover. She had uncoiled herself and was crawling rapidly toward the wounded man.

For a moment Longarm wondered what she was up to. Then he saw. She grabbed a melon-sized rock in both hands, raised it high, and with a damned good imitation of a war-whoop that naked, abused little Indian girl smashed hell out of the front of the wounded man's skull. Then she hauled the dead man's revolver out—he pretty much had to be dead after that, Longarm figured—and turned that on him.

Longarm hadn't time to watch any more. One of the live ones moved into sight, leaning out of his cover to take a shot at the girl.

Longarm fired first, and the man toppled back out of sight again.

The girl shouted something toward Longarm in her own language—but then, she wouldn't have any way to know who was up there—brandished the revolver she had captured, and charged the nest of boulders where the three men had taken cover.

Longarm could hardly believe the kid's guts. She was bareass naked and had to be hurting. She had a rock in one hand and a revolver in the other. And instead of heading for cover herself, she made a shrieking charge at three armed men.

From out of the line of Longarm's vision came three gunshots—so he hadn't killed that one he had hit, damn it—and the girl crumpled to the ground with small, damply red puckers appearing in her flesh, two of them low in the body and one of them striking her left breast. She dropped, obviously done for, and Longarm mentally apologized to her. She would not have any time left in which to grow older. Damn it.

"All right, you bastard. Now it's your turn," one of the men called defiantly. Longarm heard another gunshot, but someone was firing blind. He had no idea where the bullet went.

He tried a searching shot of his own, putting one onto a sloping rock near the men in the hope that a ricochet would get someone's attention, but he heard no yelp, so that must not have done any good. He levered a fresh shell into the chamber and reloaded the magazine of the Winchester.

"This is Deputy U.S. Marshal Custis Long, boys. I can guarantee you a fair trial if you come out peaceable."

"An' I can guarantee to shoot your fuckin' nuts off like you done to Cobb," a voice returned.

Oh, well. It had been worth a try.

He shifted to a more comfortable position and squinted up toward the sun. He had a good three hours of daylight left before the men could be expected to slip away.

The question was what to do with it. His absolutely perfect ambush spot for holding those boys under the gun when they were seated around their jug turned out to be not so damn good for getting at them now that they were armed and under cover.

A frontal assault by one man would get just about the same result that the girl had received. He might get one or even two of them but not likely all three.

He tried one more round of searching fire into the rocks, but if he hit anything, the wounded man was closed-mouthed about it.

It might very well come to an extended search, damn it. If he could not get to them before darkness they might very well sneak away. Longarm minimized their ability to travel by finding their saddle horses and sending some gravel sprays around the horses' legs. The loose stock had already disappeared as soon as the gunfire started. Now the tied horses—thank goodness they hadn't been hobbled—panicked and pulled back until they snapped their reins and took off out of sight.

"You son of a bitch," one of the men accused. He

popped into sight just long enough to throw a pistol shot in Longarm's general direction, then was behind the rocks again before Longarm had time to react with an aimed shot. The man's slug whined off the rock a good twenty yards below and to Longarm's right, doing no harm.

"I already told you there's an easier way out of this."

"Go to hell."

"After you, I expect."

There was no activity at all after that for half an hour. Longarm stayed where he was, unwilling to expose himself to the fire from below, while the three men did the same.

Sweat trickled down his sides and tickled his neck, but there was no help for that either. He had to sit it out and hope he could snag them when they tried to move.

They would have to move sometime.

While he waited and watched he studied the slope between his shelter and theirs.

It was fairly steep. That in itself was no problem, but the slope was also littered with gravel and loose rocks. If he tried to approach them he was apt to take a fall. He would have to keep his attention on their hiding place if he moved at all and would not be able to pay proper attention to the footing. With three men waiting down there to shoot him a fall would be about as bright as standing up and making a regular target of himself.

He wiped at his face and thought about the canteen hanging on one of the equipment rings of the McClellan. That didn't help anything, but he thought about it anyway.

The girl still lay where she had fallen. Her blood had mostly soaked into the gravel, but the flies were collecting on her. For some reason that bothered him, and he kept wanting to go down and shoo them away. They made no difference to Cherita, of course.

"You could still make it easy on yourselves," Longarm offered.

There was no answer. Not a sound. But if they thought

they could possum him into thinking they had already escaped, they were mistaken. It wasn't going to be that easy for them.

Longarm lifted his hat to let a little fresh air reach his scalp, checked once more to see that his magazine was full, and settled in to wait. There was nothing wrong with patience at a time like this.

A few minutes later the three rapists likely would have been willing to accept Longarm's offer of handcuffs and a jail cot.

But they no longer had the option.

He heard the approach of horses before he saw them. He assumed they were the loose horses that had run off once the shooting started, still moving around in search of their home grass.

It sounded like that, probably because these ponies too were running barefoot.

But this was a different bunch of Kiowa-Apache horses.

And these horses had Kiowa-Apache men mounted on them.

The Ka-Ays swept down the trail and burst into the clearing.

It didn't take them long to figure out the situation.

Cherita was lying there practically at their horses' feet, naked and bloody.

And the excited white men made the error of shooting. They probably could not have gotten away with hiding anyhow, but that might have given Longarm time enough to get some control over the situation.

As it was, taking a shot at eleven angry Kiowa-Apache warriors was not the smart thing to do.

That one gunshot was like putting a match to a keg of giant powder.

The Ka-Ays went into a rage, wheeling their horses almost in a single motion and charging straight on for the rocks where the men had holed up.

Longarm thought that little girl had given a pretty good war-whoop. He hadn't heard the half of it then. Now he did.

The sound of those Ka-Ay warriors was enough to chill the blood before it ever left a man's veins.

Longarm sat tight behind his boulder. He would try to get their attention when someone might be interested in listening.

One of the rapists came to his feet with his revolver leveled. Four arrows and probably that many bullets as well sent him sprawling back out of sight. He never had time to fire.

The Ka-Ays were only yards away when they started their charge. Screaming and shrieking and a couple of them chanting, they jumped off their ponies at a full run before they ever got to the rocks.

Longarm saw one Ka-Ay who had a perfectly good Kennedy repeater in his hands throw the carbine down on the ground in favor of a tomahawk that he dragged off his belt.

The two other white men stood. One of them was facing the Ka-Ays. He died before he had a chance to reach his full height when he tried to stand.

The other was running.

There was nothing but bare rock mountains behind him. The poor son of a bitch had nowhere to go, no place to hide. But he was past reasoning that out. Longarm didn't blame him.

The Ka-Ays began to yip and yelp. They sounded *happy*, by damn.

They ran after the idiot bastard, loping along behind him and grinning.

The fellow reached a slick wall of rock and tried to run up it. He got four or five feet up and fell back. The Ka-Ays were waiting for him.

"Hold it." Longarm stood and waved his arms, but no

one down there was paying any attention to him. "Damn it, don't do that." He might as well have said it to the rocks.

One of the Ka-Ays leaned down and took a little chop at the back of the man's ankle, severing his tendons so that he would not be able to use that foot again. Then the rest of them turned the fellow around and shoved him forward, inviting him to run.

The man tried. Lord knew, the man tried. He went flapping and hobbling forward on his one good foot with the other turning and twisting under him like a rag every time he tried to step on it. The Ka-Ays went with him, keeping him inside a circle of hideous faces and jabbing at him with knives and gun barrels and hatchet heads.

The man was crying. Longarm could hear him. He was bawling, calling out for someone to come help him.

He dropped down to his knees to beg the Ka-Ays for mercy, but this wasn't their day for that.

The Ka-Ay warriors quieted down and quit tormenting the poor son of a bitch when the old man called Nay-Tan came up to them. Longarm hadn't realized until that moment that Nay-Tan was with them. The warriors gave Nay-Tan some respectful silence and watched him.

The white man, down on his knees and with his trousers fouled, looked up at the old man too.

Nay-Tan said something, and the younger Ka-Ays smiled.

Longarm had been so intent on watching that he had forgotten this might be his opportunity to get their attention. He moved out into full view of them and shouted.

The Ka-Ays, Nay-Tan included, looked up and saw him there.

"Calm down now," he told them. "I am placing that man under arrest for murder and horse theft. I can 'most promise you he'll hang under the law."

Nay-Tan said something in a low voice, and the warrior

142

next to him shouted up to Longarm. "We wish to burn him. He dies slow."

"No. I have to arrest him."

The warrior said something to Nay-Tan, and the old man stood for a moment looking up at Longarm.

For just a moment there Longarm thought it was going to work.

Then Nay-Tan's arm flashed. The sharp blade of a tomahawk glittered, and the edge buried itself in the side of the white man's neck, sending a gout of blood high into the air and spraying Nay-Tan with it. It very nearly severed the man's head from his shoulders.

"You can arrest him now, Long Arm," one of the Ka-Ays called.

The Ka-Ays turned away, no longer interested in the dead man, and returned to their ponies. They gathered up Cherita's body and rode away.

Longarm supposed he had seen something of a civilized improvement there. They hadn't taken any scalps.

He shuddered. They said the Kiowa-Apache were a feisty bunch. He damn sure believed it now. And he hoped for the sake of the people of Cottonwood that Ned Sharply and old Nay-Tan never got their way about things here.

If that ever happened, it would be hell for all sides. Deputy Marshal Custis Long included.

He started slowly and carefully down the slope to check on the four dead men.

Chapter 15

Longarm was weary, worn down by frustration, not by physical exertion. Certainly his days had not been that demanding in any physical sense. But the frustrations certainly were.

Probably he should make some effort to discipline old Nay-Tan. But for what? For exacting justice against a man who had just raped and murdered a young girl?

Besides, Nay-Tan's faction among the Ka-Ays would only turn that into an excuse to declare war on the U. S. government *and* on the people of Cottonwood.

Nay-Tan and Ned Sharply would have a hell of a good time. It was everyone else, red and white alike, that Longarm was thinking about.

He grunted aloud, with only the horse to hear him. This thinking business was going to give him a headache if he didn't quit taking it so seriously. Better to have someone real to face and to fight. He would rather take on half a dozen gun rannies than try to work his way through this one.

The trouble was that he still had nothing, absolutely nothing, to go on in this case.

It was like trying to collect a pocketful of mist. He could see this; he could see that; he could grab hold of nothing at all.

Hell, maybe the worst of it was that he might very well have already killed—or seen killed—the very men who were responsible for the poisonings and therefore the so-called curse.

They could have been the gun runners, hauling poison to the water tank for reasons of their own. Reasons that might never be explained now that they were dead and beyond explanations on this side of the vale.

Or the poisoners might have been those idiots who paused in their travels for a little horse theft and rape and murder. They were far beyond discussions too.

Longarm still had no idea who those four had been or what they had been doing up here in the Guadalupes. Passing fools? That was possible, of course. It was just as possible that they were the poisoners and got themselves distracted from that just long enough to get themselves killed for their folly. There was no way to know that now.

Cobb. That was the only name of the four that he knew. The others carried nothing on them to indicate who they had been or what they had been about.

The name Cobb rang a minor bell in Longarm's memory. Just a faint tinkle, really. He thought he remembered a flier out of East Texas about a man named George Cobb who was wanted for something petty. Fence cutting, destruction of private property, something on that order. But, hell, there was no way to know if that Cobb and this one were the same man. If there had been a description on that poster, Longarm could not remember it.

Besides, after the girl bashed Cobb in the face there

hadn't been all that much left to identify him by. The whole front of the man's head had been disarranged.

So where did that leave a mystified federal deputy?

Still in the dark, that's where.

If either of those now-dead parties had been the ones he wanted, or both of them maybe connected somehow, as they were about the only ones he'd run into up here who had no logical—or at least legal—reason to be here, then he was really going to be in a pickle. James Morrison's fairy tale about a make-believe disease was not going to hold up forever. Before it went bust Longarm had to find the answer to this poisoning or they would be right back where they started and worse. The Ka-Ays and the Texans would be going to war, and Custis Long would be planted right smack in the middle of the affair.

Longarm made no attempt to follow the Ka-Ays back to the agency headquarters. Having a fuss with them over what was really a justified killing would not accomplish anything.

He found a tiny tank of sweet water, a little basin no bigger than a bushel basket tucked under an overhang of rock, and made a cold camp there.

He slept fitfully that night, worries tugging and fretting at him and interrupting his sleep. That was rare. And unwelcome.

In the morning, sitting beside his saddle with no fire to chase the night chill from his bones, he contemplated the hunk of dry, fly-tracked jerky he pulled from his saddlebag and made a sour face. Yesterday's breakfast with those young men up from Mexico had been much more palatable.

And why not a repeat of that? he asked himself. They were a pleasant bunch, young fellows out having themselves an adventure. He could always tell himself that he wanted to ask if they had seen anything or anyone suspicious in the country. The visit need not have anything to do with their coffee and refried beans. Officially.

It wasn't like he was accomplishing anything here that he would hate to interrupt.

Why not, then?

He saddled the brown and strapped his bags behind the cantle, shoving the unappetizing jerky back into the near bag.

He wasn't so far from where those boys were camped.

An hour and a half later he pulled the brown to a stop and cussed some under his breath.

The crowd of Mexican adventurers had moved on since he saw them here. There was no sign of them except for footprints and ashes.

"Well, damn," Longarm said.

The horse, the only creature likely to hear the complaint, did not care. It shook its head and dropped its muzzle to begin cropping at the few clumps of grass that were managing to survive in the arid, rocky soil.

Longarm pulled out the same chunk of unpalatable jerky and gnawed on it without interest. He washed it down with a swallow of whiskey from his carry-along bottle, and that was a little better. Finally he lighted a cheroot and sat on a handy rock to worry some more.

While he sat and smoked he automatically read the activities of the camp from the few tracks and marks left behind.

The bunch had pulled out sometime yesterday afternoon, but the depth of ashes they left behind showed that they had been here for some time.

Out of idle curiosity Longarm poked through the remains of their campfire to see how they were faring so far from home.

Pretty well, actually. Charred bone showed that they had found some fresh meat. Either an antelope from down below or a sheep. He could not tell which from only a few well-burned bones and scraps of gristle.

They preferred cornshuck cigarettes to smoking pipes or cigars.

One of them, who slept very close to the fire, spat a lot. Either sick or easily chilled, then.

They must have been running low on supplies, completely out of something, because they had burned some burlap sacks that they had carried something in.

Crazy Joe must have stayed with them more than Longarm thought from that brief conversation yesterday, because the marks of his bed were clear on the ground. He had bedded down apart from the Mexicans and in a shallow depression in a rock that was several feet short of qualifying as a cave but was a bit deeper than he would call an overhang. Longarm was pretty sure it was Joe's bed because the marks in the sand were the same as those he had found in the cave he inadvertently chased old Joe out of before, different from a bedroll, with lumps and ridges that would have made sleeping on them uncomfortable for anyone but a madman.

One of the young Mexicans liked to whittle. He left behind a partial carving that had broken at an unexpected knot in the wood. The figure would have been a rather well-made crucifix if it had been finished.

At least one of them molded his own bullets. He had dumped the dross off the skimmed top of his lead pot near the fire. There was quite a lot of it. The lead must have been unusually dirty after their travels.

One of them rode a mule. Another had a horse that needed to be re-shod. A calk had broken on the animal's off fore, and the horse was favoring that leg.

Longarm yawned, bored with the exercise now. He caught up the reins of the brown and mounted. Where to look now? And for what?

Maybe Morrison had heard something in town that

148

could help. It was the people of Cottonwood who were being threatened by the poisonings, so probably the motive should be there too.

He turned the horse toward the poisoned tank. That was the best path down to the flatlands that he knew of.

He stopped at the tainted water tank on the way down. His excuse to himself was that he wanted to see if the water had been allowed to clear. Time and constant flow would dissipate or remove the effects of the arsenates if given enough time.

The truth was that he also wanted to check on old Joe, see if the old man had made it safely back home to his cave.

It had been bothering him a little on the way down why those Mexicans, who had seemed so outgoing and friendly, had not mentioned the old fellow staying with them for an extended period. It wouldn't hurt to check the cave and see if the old man had returned to it.

What he found at the tank, though, was not good news for the people of Cottonwood.

The water in the tank was cloudy, faintly milky in appearance, although the slow flow into it from the seep seemed perfectly normal.

"Damn," Longarm muttered aloud.

He knelt and lifted a handful of the water. He did not even have to taste it to know that it had recently been laced again with a heavy application of the arsenate. He could smell the garlicky substance all too easily.

He looked for footprints that might have given him a clue to who had been here, but the surface was mostly solid rock.

"Damn," he repeated.

There was nothing to be done about it, though. Hindsight, always perfect, told him he could have kept a watch over the tank. Could have anticipated another salting of the water. Now it was too late, damn it.

Feeling frustrated and depressed again, he scrambled over the rocks until he reached the chute and began to climb up to old Joe's cave.

This time he had put a stub of candle in his pocket before he left the horse below. He lighted it when he reached the cave and went inside to check.

The cool interior of the cave was as empty now as it had been the last time he was here.

Joe had been back, though. Marks in the sandy floor showed that another bed had been made. At a different place, for some reason, this time closer to the entrance.

Longarm bent to examine it more closely.

Then, wedging the candle into a narrow crack in the rock wall, he got down on his hands and knees and began to sift through the sand with both hands, extracting and examining anything solid he found there.

When he left the cave this time he was no longer feeling so low. He was whistling and made short work of the climb back down the chute to the waiting brown.

When he remounted he turned the horse for Cottonwood.

Chapter 16

It was past noon when Longarm rode into Cottonwood. This time he made no attempt to avoid Ned Sharply's spying, or to cave in to the whims and notions of the people who followed the sassy Ranger either. He tied the brown in front of the first cafe he came to and went inside.

As before, the buzz of conversation among the few customers in the place died when he entered, but this time Longarm didn't give a damn.

"Steak," he ordered. "With fried taters. Fresh bread if you got any. Whatever else comes handy. I haven't had a decent meal in days, and I could eat a boar hog whole without stopping to wipe the mud off him first."

The girl who was waiting tables blinked, then bobbed her head. "Yes, sir, Marshal."

A few of the men in the place gave Longarm pointedly unpleasant looks, but he ignored them and they soon gave up on it.

Sharply appeared in the doorway. Either he had seen Longarm go into the cafe or someone had already told him that the federal man was back in town.

Longarm nodded to him and kicked a chair away from the table. "Sit down, Ranger Sharply. It'll be easier for you to keep an eye on me if we're together."

Sharply scowled, but he sat where Longarm indicated. He leaned his elbows on the table and gave the tall deputy a hard look. "I don't like you, Long," he said after he saw that was going to have no effect.

"That's all right, Ned," Longarm said pleasantly. "You aren't required to, far as I know."

"Damn right I don't. Fact is, Deputy, I may just decide to run your ass plumb outa Texas. We don't need you here an' we don't want you here."

"But you sure got me here."

Longarm's meal arrived, and he tucked into it with more of an appetite than he had had in days. Dry jerky couldn't hardly compare, and he was thoroughly enjoying this chance for a sit-down meal cooked by a hand other than his own.

"You might's well leave now," Sharply said while Longarm chewed on a savory piece of the tough meat. "You're fixing to be taken off this assignment anyhow. Might as well get it over with an' go."

Longarm lifted an eyebrow but continued with his meal.

"I've sent a wire to Austin. There'll be a formal complaint put in by the Attorney General o' the sov'reign state of Texas protestin' your high-handed ways. Goin' all the way up to the Attorney General of the U. S. of A., this is."

Longarm laughed. "That surely worries me, Ned. It surely does. Send Junior with the message, did you? Quite a ride to the nearest telegraph, I'd say. That should take him, what, three days to get there? Four? Then your wire has to go to Austin. Then they'll want to talk it over and see if they want to start a fuss in Washington. Then your complaint will have to be talked over there an' go out to my boss in Denver. And if I know Billy Vail, why, he'll have to talk it over with the BIA and the Interior Department." Longarm nodded. "Yeah, I'd say you might get some action on your complaint inside . . . oh, two, three months." Longarm grinned. "Maybe."

"Vail?" Sharply blurted.

"That's right. Billy Vail. Know him?"

Ned Sharply's expression was darker than ever. "Yeah, I know that sorry little son of a bitch."

Longarm laid his fork down. For the first time since Sharply arrived his demeanor was *not* pleasant. Sharply seemed too preoccupied to notice.

"I didn't think you could do it today," Longarm said softly, "but you have managed to piss me off, Ned."

That seemed to make Sharply feel better. "Why, 'cause of that shit Vail?"

"U.S. Marshal William Vail is my boss, Sharply. He is also my friend. I like him, and I respect him. That is considerable more than I can say about you." Longarm's eyes had hardened and gone cold until they looked like two shards of tempered steel, but his voice was lower and softer than ever. Again Sharply failed to see the warning signals that were flying.

"I could tell you some things about that bastard, let me tell you," he said nastily. "Why, a few years back, that little—"

It might have been an interesting, if one-sided, tale, but he never got a chance to finish it.

A fist the consistency of a small anvil flashed across the table as Longarm lunged for the man. The punch landed flush on Sharply's mouth, splitting his lips against his own teeth and knocking him backward onto the floor with blood spraying as far as the next table.

"Why, you . . ."

Sharply went for his gun, but he was not quick enough.

Longarm was already coming for him, throwing the table out from between them and charging forward.

As Sharply's Colt cleared leather, Longarm kicked his wrist and the revolver went skittering across the floor into a corner.

The way Longarm saw it—if he took the time for thought at all—was that Ned Sharply had set the rules by trying to pull iron. Anything that came to him now was of his own earning.

Longarm's boot sent the pistol flying, then lifted high and crashed down against the side of Sharply's head, tearing the Ranger's ear half away from his scalp and bloodying the man all the more.

Someone tried to rush to the popular Ranger's defense by grabbing Longarm from behind. Longarm did not see who it was and didn't give a damn. He shifted backward half a step and rammed his elbow back into the newcomer's chest. The man lost interest in the affair and turned away, gagging for breath and spewing his dinner onto the floor.

The distraction gave Sharply time enough to scramble onto his hands and knees and prepare himself for a fight.

Instead of coming for Longarm, though, he whipped a belt knife out, holding it low, point forward and edge up. The Ranger was no stranger to fighting with steel. He had lost his hat, and his hair was hanging forward over his eyes. He tossed his head to clear that away, but ignored the blood that was streaming down his neck from his mouth and ear. "You bastard," he hissed. "You're bad as that Vail."

"Just as good, too," Longarm said.

Sharply darted forward, shielding his knife hand with his left forearm, and tried to sweep the blade across Longarm's stomach.

Longarm let him come in, unhurried and judging his timing carefully. At the last possible instant he sucked his belly in. The blade of Sharply's big knife sliced through the cloth of Longarm's vest and popped a button off it but failed to reach flesh.

As soon as the knife hand was by, Longarm chopped at it with his left hand, cracking down across Sharply's wrist and numbing it. The knife clattered harmlessly to the floor, and Longarm kicked it aside.

"Now, Ranger Sharply," Longarm said softly. "You and me are gonna have a long, *long* discussion of table manners and friendships."

Longarm moved forward, and for the first time Ranger Ned Sharply began to look worried. His eyes cut back and forth, searching for the gun, for the knife. But there was nothing in reach. Nothing he could use to defend himself from the retaliation he had been asking for. His face went pale under its mask of fresh blood, and he began to back slowly toward the doorway.

But there was no place he could run. Not now.

Longarm reached for him, and Ned Sharply began to tremble.

James Morrison walked into the saloon in midafternoon, long before the school day should have ended.

Longarm was sitting by himself at a small table with a mug of beer beside him. For that matter, Longarm was sitting by himself in the entire saloon except for the bartender, who couldn't leave. He was the only customer in the place, a fact which no doubt peeved the bartender, but the man was not feeling up to asking the tall federal deputy to leave. Not today.

Longarm smiled at Morrison. "Join me if you don't mind tainting your reputation."

Morrison chuckled. "No chance of that. Fact is, a delegation came and asked me to close the school early so I could come talk to you."

"Like that, is it?"

"Like that," Morrison said with a nod.

"Can I buy you a beer, James?"

"No thanks." The schoolmaster hesitated for a moment. "Was that necessary, Longarm? You almost killed him, you know."

"His damn good fortune I stopped short of it. Come to think of it, that could be an oversight that I'll have to get around to correcting. So far the man's drawn a gun on me and then tried to knife me. I can't see a whole hell of a lot of reason to feel kindly toward him."

"Yes, well . . ." Morrison seemed unable to find any way to finish that. He let it drop and changed the subject. "Why are you here anyway, Longarm? Shouldn't you be out trying to solve our problem?"

"Already done that, I think," Longarm said, taking a swallow of the tepid beer that he had been nursing for some time. "But it will take a little work and cooperation to prove the point and bring the gentlemen in question out of the woodwork."

"You need my help?"

Longarm nodded. "Yours and that of most of the folks in town here."

Morrison smiled. "You have a strange way of trying to endear yourself to the local residents, I must say. Ned Sharply was a great favorite hereabouts."

"You're talking like the man's dead. He was and still is a total asshole. Anybody looking up to that one better do some powerful thinking about his own judgement."

Morrison shrugged. "Nevertheless . . ."

"Yeah," Longarm agreed. "Nevertheless."

"Why are you sitting in here, then?" Morrison asked.

Longarm smiled at him and took out a pair of cheroots. He offered one to Morrison, but it was declined. "Waiting for school to let out, actually. Figured I'd best talk to you first and see would you have any ideas that would help."

"All right. Tell me about it."

Longarm did. Slowly and at some length. When he was done, Morrison sat back and closed his eyes for a while to think. Finally he leaned forward and looked at Longarm again.

"It is a risk," the schoolmaster said.

"A big one," Longarm agreed.

"They would have to know," Morrison said. "About the poisoning, I mean. We would have to tell them that the disease is a hoax. They would have to know that their children have been poisoned. If this doesn't work . . . it could backfire, you know. If your plan fails, there would be no way in this world anyone would ever convince them that it was not the Indians who had done the poisonings."

"That's right," Longarm agreed.

"You're willing to take that risk?"

"Look, James, if you have a better idea, I'm willing to try it. I ain't married to the thought. If you can come up with something better, I'll damn sure go for it."

"Can I think about it for a while?"

"Be my guest. Until along about tomorrow morning, if you like. Then I ride for the reservation and start lining things up there."

"I keep thinking about the possibilities of failure," Morrison said hesitantly.

"That's all right. Divides the work load. I keep thinking about the possibilities of success," Longarm said. "Sure you don't want that beer?"

"Maybe I will at that."

Longarm left the table and took his nearly empty mug along for a refill. The bartender was slow to serve him, although he sure wasn't overrun with business at the moment.

Longarm let it go. He was not in a humor for another fight. Hell, he wished the first one hadn't happened. Like

157

Morrison had pointed out, it had done nothing to improve his likelihood of getting cooperation from the people of this town.

Besides, his right hand hurt like hell. The skin was abraded and in some places split over his knuckles, and he had a slight muscle pull in one thigh from kicking the son of a bitch.

Ned Sharply would be feeling considerably worse, though. They had carried the Ranger off, unconscious, to have the barber tend to him. He would live to ride as a Ranger again. That was something of a pity, Longarm thought, but there wasn't much he could do about the judgement of the boys back in Austin who hired Ned and thought they controlled him. Longarm did not regret a thing about the fight, damn it. Including not killing the bastard. It wouldn't have done governmental relations much good for a deputy U.S. marshal to kill a Texas Ranger.

"Ten cents," the bartender said when he'd drawn the two beers. He sounded half afraid to mention it.

Longarm rang a dime onto the polished surface of the bar and carried the mugs back to the table where James Morrison was waiting.

"If we decide to go with this idea of mine," Longarm asked, "do you think your sister would help?"

"Oh, I've little doubt about that," James said. "For that matter, she may come up with a better plan herself. She is quite a bright girl, you know."

"So I gather," Longarm said, refraining from adding that James Morrison's sister was also a hell of a looker.

"I feel sure Meaghan would help."

"Good," Longarm stubbed his cheroot out and drained off his beer. "I'll be camped behind that old barn out past your house, James. If you come up with any good ideas, you can find me there. You might pass the word to the other folks in town, though, that I won't be hosting a party over there. Anybody wants to have a word with me, he'd best come out in the open and make himself known from a distance. A man can get jumpy does someone try an' sneak up on him."

"They will stay away," Morrison assured him. "And . . . well . . . I think I can handle this end of it. If that's the way we do it, that is."

"If," Longarm said.

He left the saloon without shaking goodbye with Morrison. After all, the bartender was watching. He did not want Morrison's influence in Cottonwood undermined by more than necessary association with Custis Long, the pariah of Cottonwood.

By daybreak Morrison had come up with no better idea than Longarm's plan.

Longarm would have welcomed something better. He almost would have welcomed something simply *else*.

Like he had told Morrison, he was not so proud of his own idea that he was married to it. And he had had the whole night to think about it and worry about those possibilities of failure that James Morrison instantly saw as the fly in Longarm's ointment.

Think and worry about that, that is, whenever he was not thinking about Meg Morrison.

The memory of seeing James's sister's lithe, lovely body was haunting in the lonely night.

The girl was subtly, quietly beautiful. Sensual and enticing, yet never seeming to realize her own allure.

Damn, but she would be an armful.

He thought about her—and about the consequences for a great many people if he should fail now—almost through to the dawn, but when Morrison came to talk with him Longarm was saddled and ready to go.

This morning he settled for dry jerky and stagnant water from the surface pool for his breakfast. He did not want any repeats of yesterday's troubles in the cafe.

"Well?" he asked Morrison without preamble.

The schoolmaster, who looked like he had slept even less than Longarm during the night, shook his head. "I can't think of anything that would be better."

"All right, then. We go with it. You know what to do?"

Morrison nodded. He did not look happy, but he nodded.

Longarm mounted the brown and reached down from the saddle to shake Morrison's hand.

"Good luck," he said solemnly.

"And to you."

Both men looked grim when they parted.

As he rode, Longarm kept thinking that much, so very much, depended now on the good will of George O'Hara.

And on that of the strange and bloodthirsty old man they called Nay-Tan.

He shivered as he thought of it. But that, perhaps, was only because the sun was not yet high enough to warm that chill spot between his shoulder blades.

Chapter 17

Longarm was in the saloon. The barman had managed to come up with a bottle of Pennsylvania rye whiskey, which was welcome. It did not relieve any of the worries he'd been having since he got back from the Kiowa-Apache reservation, but it warmed his belly some.

You would think that in a hot country like this there should be no trouble keeping warm. For the past couple of days here, Longarm had had plenty of trouble trying to warm himself. At least inside. His digestion was no good. No kind of food seemed to sit well on his stomach, and he couldn't sleep worth a damn.

And every damn night as he lay awake he insisted, in spite of his best resolve, on thinking about Meg Morrison.

Funny, he thought, how she was Meg in his mind when he was wanting her, Meaghan when he was talking with her brother. Or maybe not so funny.

Damn, but he wanted that one. But at the reservation

161

she'd been all business. Cooperative and polite and willing to do whatever she could to help with Longarm's plans, but distant.

He kept trying to tell himself that she was just shy, as he'd guessed that night when he saw her leaving her bath. But now he wasn't so sure of that.

She couldn't, just couldn't be one of those females that likes other women. Just couldn't. A trick like that would be just too cruel, even for uncaring Nature.

Whatever it was, Meg Morrison hadn't given him any of those signs or signals that lets a man know she is interested in him. Not a one. She'd just been polite and pleasant and agreeable . . . and distant.

Thinking about Meg these past couple of days hadn't helped him any, although it gave him opportunities to think about something other than all the thousands of things that could go wrong.

Longarm raised his glass and took a short swallow of the good rye.

There were other men in the place tonight. They weren't being especially friendly to him, but he didn't feel like he had to watch his backside with anything more than normal caution, either. Maybe that was an improvement of sorts.

He drained the whiskey off and wandered out onto the sidewalk to lean against the wall of the saloon. The night air was clear and pleasingly cool after the intense heat of the day. Off toward the Pecos the moon was lifting over the horizon.

Longarm watched it climb. Moon or sun either one, when they were overhead they seemed to just hang there. But down close to the ground you could see that they moved right along.

He could see some bats flitting their erratic course between him and the moon. He had no idea if the bats came to the water in the pool in the bend because they wanted to drink or if they were just after the insects that would be swarming at the water. It was something he should remember to ask someone sometime.

At least he told himself that. It was something to think about other than his worries and other than Meg Morrison.

Off to the east the moon lifted clear of the horizon.

And off to the west there was the sudden thump and rattle of gunfire, followed quickly by the soul-chilling sounds of Kiowa-Apache war-whoops.

Longarm's stomach began to churn as he turned and bolted for the west end of Cottonwood with the townspeople spilling out of the saloons and their homes, men shouting and carrying their guns, the women and children running in all directions and screaming.

Oh, Lordy, Longarm thought.

The Ka-Ays swept in in waves. Longarm hadn't thought there were so many Kiowa-Apaches in the world, much less up on that mostly empty reservation. Hell, they must have called in their kinfolk from hundreds of miles around to gather that many horses and that many screaming, yelping, hideously painted warriors.

They boomed drums and fired guns of every size and description, likely, that had been manufactured since white men first hit the continent—and maybe some that were older than that, too—and shook rattles and waved lances and yelped and hollered like crazy men. Which, in a way, they looked like they were.

The older ones had even brought along their scalp lances and were brandishing those while they charged Cottonwood, Texas.

The warriors were painted to look like demons—which in a way they were—and the youngsters not old enough to have scalps on their lances looked like they were damn sure ready to start a collection right now.

Longarm grabbed out his Colt and set it to bellowing, and all around him the people of Cottonwood were taking cover or some of them just standing in the middle of the street at the west end of town and firing as hard and fast as they could reload.

Muzzle flashes and powder smoke turned the night into a hellfire-and-brimstone scene of man-made mists and artificial lightning. In all his days Longarm had never seen the like of it.

Women were screaming and clutching their breasts, and children were skittering underfoot like so many chicks turned loose in a coop and a snake tossed into the middle of them.

Some half-mad Indian—the light was poor, but Longarm thought it was old Nay-Tan—was carrying a torch, and a bunch of the younger Ka-Ays lit fire arrows from that and began shooting those toward the townspeople.

The flaming arrows looked like shooting stars against the night sky. They thumped into the side of the old barn, and the dry wood caught and commenced to burn, throwing flickering firelight over that whole end of town.

A few of the things fell short and set the brown grass afire, adding that much more flame and smoke to the confusion.

A tight bunch of the young Ka-Ays, naked except for paint and breechclouts and armed with lances and war clubs, broke through the line of defenders and thundered the length of the street on sweating, straining ponies that had been maddened by the turmoil and the excitement of their riders. The sounds of breaking glass were added to the gunfire and the shrieks.

Oh, hell, Longarm thought. *Please, no*.

A Texan ran forward, screaming as loud as any Indian and waving his empty rifle like a club. "Stop it. Stop it, you sons of bitches," he shouted.

Longarm dashed after him, grabbed him by the collar of his coat, and hauled him back to the rest of the Texans, who had formed a human breastworks across that end of the street and were continuing to pour fire toward the Ka-Ays.

Longarm had forgotten about that idiot Ned Sharply. The lean Ranger, battered and his face still mottled purple from the bruises Longarm had put on him, came wobbling out from wherever they'd put him to recover. He had a brace of revolvers, one in each shaky hand.

Longarm saw him and immediately went for him, tackling him around the waist and wrestling him to the ground.

Sharply screamed his outrage and tried to squirm into position to fire past Longarm's shoulder while he lay on the ground with Longarm trying to grab the guns away from him.

One of the townspeople came running up and gave Longarm a hand, twisting the guns out of Sharply's fingers and shoving them behind his own belt.

"What the fuck . . . ?"

Longarm let go of Sharply and got to his feet again. He reloaded his revolver and emptied the cylinder into the night.

A few yards away the waves of Kiowa-Apache warriors continued to wheel in a circle, sweeping in close to the Texans to scream and taunt and fire their guns.

"Helluva night for a gunpowder salesman," Longarm muttered to the man who had helped him disarm Sharply.

"Ain't that the truth." The Texan pulled Sharply's revolvers and emptied them as quickly as he could work through the cylinders.

He and Longarm both reloaded and shot again.

In front of them the war cries were louder than ever, and the Ka-Ay gunfire was fierce. The roof of the barn caught with a whoosh of flame loud enough to make itself heard over all the other noise, and sparks soared in a golden column into the moonlit sky. Most of the Cottonwood women ran for buckets of water to keep the embers from touching off other buildings, but the menfolk continued to shoot toward the demon Ka-Ays.

Chapter 18

Dawn found the streets of Cottonwood silent and deserted. Tomblike.

The charcoal and ash that remained of the old barn continued to smoulder, sending a pall of smoke across the scene of the battle and along with it the stink of dew-damp char.

Bodies, white men and red alike, littered that end of town like so many piles of cast-off rags, their weapons beside or beneath them.

Longarm lay face down behind the breastworks of the old well behind what was left of the barn, his Colt in his hand and the Winchester nearby.

A puff of breeze came with the dawn, making the low-hanging smoke swirl and eddy above and among the bodies.

Indian war ponies, painted as gaudily as their riders had been, grazed riderless now on the flat above the dry creekbed, some of them patiently standing with their single horsehair reins clutched in the hands of the warriors who had ridden them to the attack.

The smoke and the nervously shifting ponies provided the only movement in sight.

Except for them, the town of Cottonwood seemed utterly lifeless.

Before the sun had cleared the eastern horizon there was a metallic rattle of bits and spurs from down in the creekbed. Riders came slowly into view, popping up over the lip of the bank cautiously, waiting there for a while to survey the scene in Cottonwood.

They climbed the bank only far enough for them to see over it, then stopped. After a minute or two someone spoke in a commanding voice, and the several dozen riders came on, spurring their horses the last few yards to the level ground, then stopping there again.

They rode forward as a tight group, their horses curveting and nervous from the strange scents around them.

The man in the lead grinned and said something to his companions. Several of them laughed. All of them seemed to relax and to sit lighter and easier in their platter-horned saddles.

"Aiiee. Es bueno, no?" the lead man said, still grinning.

The riders moved forward again, riding past the flattened, smouldering barn and into the heaps of bodies.

"Now," another voice called out in a quiet but firm tone.

Longarm stirred and came to his feet. His Colt was still in his fist and leveled now toward Juan Cardenas and his Mexican adventurers.

Adventurers, indeed.

All around the riders, the dead arose.

Texan and Kiowa-Apache alike stood.

Texan and Kiowa-Apache alike held weapons pointing into the circle they had created around the Mexicans.

168

Alarm wiped the grin off Cardenas's face. He spun his horse in a quick circle, but he and his men were surrounded by the live fighters he had thought were dead.

Too late he would have been able to see that there was no blood in the dust. There were no women or children anywhere in sight. Every woman and every child of Cottonwood and its immediate surroundings were hiding in basements.

Longarm walked toward the shocked Mexicans.

"Morning, Juan. Gentlemen."

"But . . ." Cardenas's eyes were wide with disbelief and confusion.

Longarm smiled at him. "That little deal we put on last night? Just playing, Juan. We were just playing and wanting to see who else came to our party."

"But . . . but . . ."

"I kinda thought it would be your bunch, Juan, but I wasn't positive. Sorry to see I was right, actually. I really thought you were a nice bunch of fellas."

Cardenas's eyes hardened. "This is our land. Not these greedy Tejanos's. Not these stinking savages. Ours. Our fathers' an' ours. It belongs to us. They should not have it."

"Is that reason enough to poison babies?" Longarm asked.

Cardenas's eyes shifted away from his at the mention of that. "It was not . . ." He shut up.

"I know. That wasn't your idea, was it? But you went along with it, Juan. That makes you just as guilty as the next fellow. Speaking of the next fellow, where is he?

Cardenas shook his head stubbornly. He still would not meet Longarm's eyes.

His men were becoming more and more nervous. At the talk of poison and babies, the circle of gunmen around them hardened, the Texans in particular taking fresh grips on their weapons. Many of the Texans and more than a few of the Ka-Ays, who had considerably more feeling for any child, white or red, than they would have for, say, a puppy, began to move in, tightening the circle around the Mexicans, while they tightened their holds on their rifles and revolvers.

One of the young Mexicans, the same handsome young man who had brought Longarm his plate of beans the other morning, could not stand the strain or the threats he could see in the eyes of the Anglos and the Ka-Ays around him. He broke and with a cry of anguish rammed steel rowels into the flanks of his horse.

The horse bolted forward, wringing its tail in pain.

The animal had not had time to take more than a few steps before its pain was relieved and its rider gone, smashed out of his saddle by a loud, harsh volley of gunfire and shot through the chest as well by a fistful of feathered arrows.

"Hold it," Longarm snapped.

The Mexicans were frantically trying to hold their horses quiet. A sudden movement, no matter whose fault or what the intention, would be their last, and they knew it.

"Ease off now," Longarm said in a low voice just loud enough to carry to the men around him. "Everybody set easy."

The dead Mexican's horse ran bucking and snorting back down into the creekbed, but no one was paying any attention to it. All eyes were on the outnumbered and outgunned band of frightened raiders from south of the border.

"What . . . ?" Cardenas licked dry lips "What will you do now?"

"First thing, I want you boys to take turns. One at a time I want you to shed your weapons, ride forward about ten yards, and dismount so we can tie you. You don't have to do that, of course, but you know what'll happen if you choose not to. You understand me, Juan?"

Cardenas nodded. "*Sí.* I understand."

"Good. You can be first."

Cardenas hesitated. "What will be done? You know."

Longarm shrugged. "Matter of fact I don't know. Funny as it may sound, Juan, poisoning babies isn't a violation of federal law. My part in it will be to turn you over to local authority. If I had to guess, I'd say that you'll hang. But that isn't up to me."

They would hang, Longarm guessed, if they lived long enough to go to trial. With Ned Sharply as the local law there was some question about that, but it was not something Longarm was going to worry about a whole hell of a lot. It would be difficult to work up much in the way of sympathy or compassion for anyone who poisoned infants. And Longarm hadn't hired on to police the whole world, just to do what he reasonably could.

Cardenas shuddered. He looked at the Texans and the Indians who surrounded him. What he saw could not have been reassuring. His shoulders slumped in resignation and he very slowly and carefully eased his horse forward, dismounted, and allowed himself to be bound.

If he could have seen what Longarm saw he might have chosen to go out quickly in a burst of gunfire.

At least that would have been swift and sure.

Behind the Mexicans, Longarm could see some of the women of Cottonwood coming out of hiding and moving forward to take a look at the men who were responsible for the deaths of those children.

If Cardenas could have seen what Longarm saw in those hooded, hateful eyes, he could never have exposed himself to the possibility that the women of Cottonwood might seek their own home-rolled version of justice once Longarm's back was turned.

Cardenas and his men would get neither charity nor quarter from the ladies of Cottonwood.

But whether the women were allowed to take the prisoners or not would be on Ned Sharply's conscience, not Custis Long's.

One by one the raiders surrendered to the Texans and their Kiowa-Apache allies.

Longarm holstered his Colt and headed for the other end of town where he had left the brown.

"You leave, Long Arm?" It was George O'Hara. O'Hara had been the leader of the "attacking" party of Ka-Ays. The council president must have had a hell of a lot of talking to do to convince the Ka-Ays to join forces with the Texans in the deception, but he had handled it. That had taken place after Longarm and Meg Morrison convinced him and left the council decision in his hands. Until moonrise last night, Longarm had not been sure himself that the false raid would be carried out. He still marveled that they had managed to do it without real bloodshed on either side.

"I still have work to do, George. These boys figured to reap the benefit if they could get you and the folks of Cottonwood to go to war. But they weren't the ones who thought it up. Not like this. They wouldn't have had the know-how for this plan."

"You will be back, Long Arm?"

"I'll be back. I don't figure to be alone."

"Come to the reservation. We will feast in your honor."

Longarm smiled at him. "When you do, I'd take it kindly if you could get old Wah-to-Nah-Tah to lift that curse he put on the Texans. I haven't told anybody that they'd really been cursed, but still . . ."

O'Hara's eyes widened in surprise for a moment. Then he smiled. "Farady does not know."

"Long Arm does. Like I said, I'd take it kindly if you could get that old scoundrel to lift his curse. I mean, I don't believe in curses or anything. But still . . . it wouldn't hurt to have it lifted. Just in case."

172

"You guessed?" the Ka-Ay asked.

"Uh-huh. I guessed. It's the sort of thing Nay-Tan would do. He's a mean bastard."

O'Hara shrugged. "Wah-to-Nah-Tah follows the Way. As I would wish to if the world was younger, Long Arm."

"But the world isn't younger, George. We all have to live in the one we're given."

"It is what I try to tell my people, and myself, each day."

"You'll make it, George. You and your people got a good head start on that here last night and this morning."

"Yes, and that is good. The Great Spirit sometimes hides good things in dark places."

"I'll see you again before I leave, George. We'll have a drink and a smoke and talk about a younger world."

"Yes, Long Arm. We will do those things. And I shall speak with Nathan many times before you come."

Longarm smiled at him and headed for his horse. The Mexicans were being led away.

Finding the mastermind behind the poisonings was not easy. A man on foot leaves damn little sign in country as rough as the Guadalupes. It took Longarm three days to catch up with him, and then it was more by luck than by logic. A wisp of smoke curling out of a tiny fissure in the rock gave him away, and at that it took Longarm several more hours of searching before he finally found the cave entrance around on the other side of that particular formation and a hundred feet lower in elevation.

The opening was tiny, barely wide enough for a human to wriggle into, but a few feet into the rock it opened into a cavern larger than most barns.

The man's fire had been built at the left rear of the cavern, beneath a natural chimney that gave ventilation and cleared the smoke by rising through that fissure Longarm had spotted in the sunlight far above.

The man looked at Longarm and cackled. "Did you bring ol' Joe some peaches."

"Cut the bullshit, Franklyn. I came to arrest you."

Un-crazy Joe's expression hardened, and he stood taller and straighter than Longarm had seen him before.

"What went wrong?" he asked.

Longarm shrugged. He was looking around the cavern. The firelight filled the place adequately, reflecting off the pale stone that surrounded it. It was fixed up to be fairly comfortable, with a crude but decent enough bed built in one corner and several trunks spotted around like chairs. Off to the right there was a pile of plump burlap sacks of the size that might have held fifty pounds of flour apiece. These particular sacks, Longarm was sure, each held fifty pounds of death. There were only six of the sacks left, but marks in the sand beside them showed that there had been a good many more piled there at one time. The marks looked very much like those of a long bed but with long, thin lines cross-hatching the "bed" where the sacks had not quite joined when they were laid side by side.

Spikes had been driven into the rock walls here and there to hold stored cooking utensils, an old-fashioned but very well-made suit of formal clothes, and a Sharps buffalo rifle in one of the exceptionally large calibers.

"You won't tell me?" Franklyn asked.

"Oh, I don't mind telling you." Longarm pulled out a cheroot and lighted it. Belatedly he thought to offer one to his prisoner. Franklyn accepted, although with a frown at the quality after he first tasted the smoke. He was accustomed to better than a federal deputy could afford. "Would you mind telling me a few things, though?"

"Probably not," Franklyn said. The old man seemed perfectly at ease. He settled on one of the trunks and crossed his legs.

Longarm explained it to him briefly. The marks he had first thought to have been beds. The burnt burlap sacks at the Mexicans' campfire just about the time the water tank was poisoned again. The fact that the Mexican adventurers might have an axe to grind with the people who had displaced them at San Felipe de Avila.

"What I don't understand," Longarm said, "is what you figured to get out of it. You almost had to be behind it, but I still don't know why."

Franklyn chuckled. "They told you about me, did they?"

"Didn't have to," Longarm said. "Pretty much had to be you. You went heavy into the buffalo hide business right when the buffalo played out. One of the things lead arsenate is used for is preserving hides to keep them from rotting while they're being shipped for tanning."

"Sodium, " Franklyn said.

"Sir?"

"Sodium arsenate, not lead. It was my good fortune to have purchased the sodium arsenate. The price was lower for it than the lead when I bought years ago."

"What difference does that make?"

"The lead arsenate is not so readily soluble in cold water. Sodium arsenate is."

Longarm grunted and drew on his cheroot. "You still haven't told me why you were using those Mexicans, what you figured to get out of it."

"Couldn't you simply accept it as an act of charity toward a displaced people?" Franklyn asked with a smirk.

"Kinda hard to think of killing babies as an act of charity, Franklyn. No, I'd say you had a plan to gain from this."

"And so I do," Joe said. "It's simple, really. Create dissension between the settlers and the Indians—those damned Kiowa-Apache almost killed me once up on the Llano, you know; did murder my gun and skinning crews or I might yet have had time to recapture my fortunes—and the Texans . . ." He shrugged. "What I have seen of them convinces me they are all fools anyway."

"Compared to you," Longarm said drily. Hell, Joe Franklyn *was* as crazy as Longarm had thought to begin with. Just in a different way, was all.

"Exactly," Franklyn agreed seriously. "My intention has always been to have one group eliminate the other. Then I could move in and repopulate the area with docile, eminently leadable men like Cardenas and his sluggish companions." Franklyn seemed quite pleased with himself.

"Leadable," Longarm repeated slowly. "You would do the leading yourself, I take it."

"But of course, my dear fellow. No one else would be qualified for the task. They require direction. I would give it to them."

Longarm chewed on that for a moment. "You arranged to have those guns brought in for your troops?"

"Of course. I need an army, don't you see. One cannot have an army without arms." Franklyn was smiling broadly. "For that matter, my dear fellow, I shall be requiring law enforcement also. The position is open, if you understand my meaning." He winked at Longarm.

"You figure to set up your own damn country, don't you?" Longarm said. It was an incredible notion that he was forced to give credibility, at least as to intent.

"But of course, my dear fellow. The Free State of Franklyn. Joseph Franklyn, president. Or possibly monarch. I have not yet decided how I shall style myself at the inauguration. Which do you think?"

The old bastard certainly sounded serious. Longarm could not quite decide if Franklyn was really this crazy or only trying to make Longarm believe that he was.

"While you are thinking about that," Franklyn said happily, "you should give some thought to your own title. Minister of Internal Security might be good. It carries a certain distinction. Much more so, I think, than Chief of National Police Forces." Franklyn squinted and cocked his head to one side while he gave Longarm a long, speculative look. "I might even consider appointing you the head of my armed forces as well. You have an air of competence that could be greatly useful to me, General Long."

So the old bastard remembered Longarm's name perfectly well. He couldn't be crazy. Or could he? "You don't think the United States government will mind losing the ground for the Free State of Franklyn?"

"Not enough to fight a war over. After all, I only intend to take the area between the Pecos and the Rio Grande, from Sierra Blanca south. It is poor land, hardly worth fighting over. They shall never miss it." He smiled. "Believe me, General Long, I have considered this quite carefully. I have old and dear friends in positions of great influence in England and France and Holland. A few even in Prussia. Once they accept the sovereignty of Franklyn as a free and independent nation, I shall have a fait accompli. The United States shall have no choice but to accept Franklyn as a neighbor and ally."

"President," Longarm said.

"Come again?"

"I think you should call yourself president of Franklyn. It would sit better with the U. S. than making yourself out to be a king. Americans have never been all that fond of kings, you know."

Franklyn beamed. He clapped his thigh with an open palm and chortled, "Excellent advice, General Long. Exactly the sort of thing I hired you for."

"Yes, but right now, President Franklyn, I believe you and I should go down and review your troops. They are waiting for you in Cottonwood."

Franklyn looked horrified. "Please, General. I promised my people that that name should be heard no more. We much prefer San Felipe. Although, of course, if I choose to make it my capital city the name must be changed to Franklyn."

"Of course, Mr. President. My apologies. Would you please accompany me, then? Your people need you to lead them."

"Delighted, General. I shall be delighted to appear for my people." Smiling, Franklyn stood and strode to the spike where his best clothes had been left. The coat was a split-tail morning coat. He took it down and brushed it carefully before he put it on over his filthy crazy-Joe rags. He was smiling.

Longarm turned toward the entrance to the cave.

He glanced back toward Joseph Franklyn in time to see that the man was not half as daft as he wanted people to believe.

Franklyn had an old percussion derringer in a pocket of the coat. He was in the process of trying to get it cocked and aimed at the center of "General" Custis Long's back.

Affairs of state might have been Franklyn's forte, but dealing with backshooters was one of Longarm's. Longarm's Colt roared inside the confinement of the cavern, putting a ringing in Longarm's ears and bringing a cascade of rock dust down onto his shoulders.

The Colt also put a hole in Joseph Franklyn's chest big enough to bury the Free State of Franklyn in.

"Damn it," Longarm said aloud although the concussion had pressed so strongly on his ears that he could not hear his own voice.

Now he never would know how much of that stuff Crazy Joe had believed himself and what part of it was just for show.

"Damn it," he said again.

Chapter 19

Longarm buried Joseph Franklyn in the cavern where he had lived the last years of his odd life, then sealed off the tiny entrance as best he could with boulders. No one was likely to find the opening or to realize that it led to the cave if they did find it. The cavern would probably serve as Crazy Joe's crypt for all time, holding not only the remains of Joseph Franklyn but also the remains of his dreams.

If the true dreams those had been. When he thought back on the conversation, it occurred to him that Franklyn may very well have been parroting back Longarm's own guesses and expanding on them. His real purposes might never be known. Or they as easily might be those that Franklyn talked so freely about in his last minutes.

It bothered Longarm that he would never know for sure what the truth was, but there was no help for that now.

He put it out of his mind and rode north to the Kiowa-Apache reservation.

Things were peaceful there, and George O'Hara believed there was a strong chance that they could remain so. Nathan, the last war chief of the Kiowa-Apache, had gone into a sulk. Longarm did not see him again except in the picture that hung next to George Washington's in the Ka-Ay schoolhouse.

The schoolhouse was empty. Meg Morrison was taking some time to stay with her brother down in Cottonwood.

Longarm could not help thinking that Meg might be hoping he would come back there once his mission was ended. He still kept thinking that perhaps she was shyly hopeful that they would have some private moments before he left. After only a few days of drinking and feasting with O'Hara and the other Ka-Ay council leaders, he saddled the brown and took the road southeast toward Cottonwood.

He detoured west when he reached the flat grass country to check on the tank that fed Cottonwood's water supply.

The water still smelled of garlic, but neither the odor nor the flavor were strong. In time the water would clear and the people of Cottonwood could quit hauling their drinking water from the Pecos. That would be a relief for them, not only because of the labor involved, but because the Pecos water was usually alkaline and unpleasant to drink.

There was no sign of Ned Sharply or of the Mexican prisoners in Cottonwood. No one volunteered to tell him what had happened to them, and Longarm refrained from asking. Hell, maybe Sharply was a better lawman than Longarm was giving him credit for being. Maybe the Ranger was taking the prisoners east for trial and hanging.

Or maybe they were already buried.

Longarm did not want to put himself in the position of having to judge the actions of people who had lost children and whose living children had been threatened with death.

Whatever they had or had not done, it was something that they would have to live with, not he.

He ate a good meal at the cafe and saw to the needs of the horse, then walked to James Morrison's place after dark.

This evening could be awkward if James was at home. But if James happened to be elsewhere for the evening . . .

There was no immediate answer to his knock, although there was a low-trimmed lamp burning at the window on the left side of the adobe house. He knocked again.

His third rap was answered, and Meg stood before him.

She had carried a candle with her. It provided the only light in the front room of the house, and she was beautiful in that light.

She wore the robe he had seen her use that other night after her bath. Her face was flushed prettily, her cheeks red and her breath coming in quick, hard gasps. She looked . . . But that was impossible.

Still, she must be here alone. There was no sign of James.

She looked at him in stunned silence, and Longarm concluded that she must have been thinking about him when she worked herself into that solitary state.

She definitely had the look of a woman interrupted in a throe of passion. The flushed cheeks, the hard breathing, the dew of moisture between her breasts where the robe gapped at the front . . . it all fit. He smiled and stepped inside.

A scent of French perfume surrounded her.

Meg had prepared herself for loving and had no one to give it to her except herself.

Longarm reached for her, putting an arm gently around her shoulders.

Her reaction was not what he expected.

Meg yelped as if he had struck her. She slapped him

hard across the face and backed away, holding the candle in one hand and clutching at the front of the robe with the other.

At the sound a door off the front room smashed open, and James came rushing out to help her.

James was barefoot. He had wrapped a towel around his waist but otherwise he appeared to be naked. And he was every bit as sweaty and flushed as Meaghan was.

He stopped short when he saw who the intruder was.

Meaghan—Longarm had all of a sudden quit thinking of her as Meg again—began to cry. She turned and buried her face against her brother's naked chest.

Her brother's naked, sweaty chest.

Longarm stood rooted where he was. He felt the fool. And worse.

But her brother?

James looked embarrassed. Meaghan continued to cry. James wrapped his arms protectively around her and held her to him, rocking back and forth silently as he stared across her head at Longarm.

James petted Meaghan for a moment, stroking her hair and holding her. He kissed the top of her head, patted her again, and moved her toward the open door. He gave her a little push and sent her inside the bedroom of the tiny house, then closed the door and turned to face Longarm.

His look now was anything but gentle. "Well?" he demanded.

"I'm sorry." It was all Longarm could think to say. It was certainly the truth. "I didn't mean . . ."

"Are you going to arrest us?"

"No." Longarm felt an overwhelming sadness. For James. For Meaghan. For himself. He was not sure he could have said for whom just then. For all of them, probably. "No, of course not."

"We have violated the law, I suppose," James said. He

sounded angry. Possibly with himself and with his sister as much as he was with Longarm.

"I suppose you have," Longarm said. "But that's God's law, not the U. S. government's. Nobody's ever told me I had to enforce those laws."

"Are you going to . . . ?" Morrison could not finish the question.

"No," Longarm said sadly. "I'll not be spreading gossip. You can have little enough happiness as it is. I'll not be the one to deny you what there is of it."

Morrison nodded. He looked like he was about to weep.

"I just . . . I just came to tell you goodbye," Longarm said. It sounded weak even to him, but it would have to do.

"All right."

"Tell your . . . sister for me, please. And give her my apologies. I didn't mean to frighten her."

Morrison nodded again.

The two men stood silently looking at each other for a moment. Longarm spread his hands and started to speak. But there was nothing more to be said.

He turned and let himself out of the tiny adobe, pulling the door shut behind him.

The night air felt cool. Cleansing. He looked toward the moon rising to the east.

In the other direction was El Paso. If he started now he could get a good many miles toward it before the brown horse needed rest again.

There would be lights in El Paso, and people. Maryland rye whiskey and a train connection the long way around back to Denver.

With luck, maybe his old acquaintance Linda Bayliss was still living there. He would have to inquire after her.

Longarm tugged the brown Stetson low on his brow and walked quickly back toward where he had left the horse. There were no leave-takings he had to make in Cottonwood. None but the one he wished he had not had to make already.

But, hell, tomorrow would be better.

He was almost in a fair humor by the time he pulled the cinch of the McClellan tight and stepped into the saddle.

The rising moon shed a peaceful light over Cottonwood as Longarm turned away from it and from the town and headed the horse southwest toward El Paso.

Watch for

**LONGARM AND THE DESPERATE
MANHUNT**

one hundred and second novel in the bold
LONGARM series from Jove

coming in June!

Explore the exciting Old West with one of the men who made it wild!